The Head of Alvise

The Head of Alvise

To be or to have
But to be I must have
The head of Alvise
On a silver platter

Lina Wertmüller

William Morrow and Company, Inc.
New York   1982

Originally published in Italy by Rizzoli Editore under the title *La testa di Alvise*

All rights reserved. No part of this book may be reproduced or utilized in any form or by any means, electronic or mechanical, including photocopying, recording or by any information storage and retrieval system, without permission in writing from the Publisher. Inquiries should be addressed to William Morrow and Company, Inc., 105 Madison Avenue, New York, N.Y. 10016.

Library of Congress Cataloging in Publication Data

Wertmüller, Lina.
  The head of Alvise.

  Translation of: La testa di Alvise.
  I. Title.
PQ4883.E7T413   853'.914   82–3528
ISBN 0–688–01124–1   AACR2

Printed in the United States of America

First Edition

1 2 3 4 5 6 7 8 9 10

BOOK DESIGN BY BERNARD SCHLEIFER

Acknowledgments

I wish to thank Arrigo Colombo, Carlo Tagliacozzo and Nora Hoppe for the assistance they gave me in this adventure, and Caterina Zaccaroni and Lydia Lundry for their help in the translation.

The shortest distance between two points
is the arabesque.

—ENNIO FLAIANO

The Head of Alvise

Prologue

Andante Avventuroso

"IF I COULD ONLY HAVE . . . a thousand lire a month. . . ."

The gondola glides over the green waters of the lagoon. The lyrics of the song croaking on the radio mingle with the lively voices of the crowds as they stroll over bridges, along lanes and through piazzas.

Pa pricks up his ears at the mention of money.

"Well, these Italians . . . a thousand lire a month. Wages, Money . . . At least they write songs about serious things, instead of all that crap about the moonlight and 'I can't give you anything but love, baby,' like us in America."

Sprawled in the back of the gondola, he shakes his head and puts the cigar in his mouth.

Sunshine, statues, graceful bridges suspended over canals, churches rising from the waters. Venice, 1939.

Venice! Fabulous pearl of the Adriatic, the bride of the sea.

And what are the mullioned windows? They are jewels.

And what are the palazzi? They are lace hewn out of stone.

And what are the gondoliers? Handsome, strapping Italian youths who look like movie stars.

And what is Piazza San Marco with its orchestras? A salon.

Venice. The Merchant of Venice. Death in Venice. The Carnival in Venice. The Mysteries of Venice.

If it weren't stupendous it would be kitsch.

The lagoon and the sounds of guitars. Gondolas and the posters for the 1939 film festival.

And the waves that break elegantly over the beach of the Lido.

The tents. The bathing cabins. The handsome lifeguards in striped shirts and straw hats.

The beach chairs for sunbathing. The hot summer sun.

The beach umbrellas. And far in the distance, sailboats on the light blue sea.

The art-nouveau elegance of the Excelsior Hotel.

A blond angel, smiling and cordial, with windblown hair, golden against the light, a young Prince Charming or Little Lord Fauntleroy, who holds out his hand to me.

"Sam. Your name is Sam. What a nice name. My name is Alvise."

And I, sweaty, skinny, peeling and blistered, with a huge sunburnt nose, wearing a scruffy tank top and a pair of cheap sandals, look at him and wrinkle my nose.

"Alvise. How stupid. Alvise. What kinda name is that?"

"My grandfather's name."

Alvise . . . get it? Already someone with a name like Alvise is something special. You can imagine him in his cradle, with all the relatives around. In the beginning of the century—let's say around the early twenties, which now seem so elegant as to make us yearn with nostalgia. In a cathedrallike bedroom. Very very very aristocratic! One of those awesome strongholds that belong to the rich. An intimate place for aristocratic birthing. A very chic group of relatives standing around a dazzling bed of snow-white lace, pinnacles, spires, ruffles, tulle and feather pillows. An extremely elegant gentleman, overcome by emotion, observes the infant, wrapped in delicate lace coverlets, and tucked in the arms of a prim and starched nurse.

"We shall name him Alvise, after his grandfather . . ."

And so, you meet on the beach of the Venice Lido, Hotel Excelsior, a kid named Alvise. So handsome and so elegant, and who smiles at you.

Well, right away my big nose sensed something fishy, and my childish suspicions were soon confirmed.

I don't know if you realize . . . We both said Mamma. I mean, he said Mamma and I said Mamma. The word was the same, right? But Alvise's mother was a lady, exquisite, aristocratic, diaphanous, elegant; white veils fluttered around her like ballerinas dancing *Swan Lake*. She opened her mouth, and out would come butterflies and the sounds of harps and violins. She had silken hair and magical, mysterious hats, made of flowers, birds of paradise, veils and stars. Her skin was whipped cream. And her hands were snow-white flowers.

While my mother . . . well, I know. It isn't right to criticize your mother. Poor dear, but it isn't to be critical. My mom was even nice. But fat, with enormous and colorful bags, cheap sandals, dresses full of loud stripes and flowers, crooked little straw hats. She was a typical American tourist. And she too had a fleshy, red, sweaty, peeling and sunburnt nose.

As for that aristocratic gentleman Alvise called Papa, he dressed impeccably in a white linen suit with a fabulous panama.

My papa, of course, had the same *putz*-face that I do, stuck on a squat, chunky, mercantile body, supported by two short, crooked legs. He was a typical New York Jew, in the jewelry business, marked by a vulgar and elevated quotient of avidity.

I mean . . . I don't know, pretentiously I would talk about our "villa," referring to the one Papa had rented. It was a *schmaltzy* middle-class bungalow, surrounded by many like it. A lousy shack, with a slovenly maid, and a one-square-foot backyard.

And Alvise said: "We have a villa too."

Except that he was talking about the "Ombreggiata." Which was a sort of marble miracle set at the end of a long, tree-lined driveway, on a luxurious green island in the lagoon. A magnificent antique Venetian villa, with an eight-columned portico built by a certain Palladium.

An enormous villa which seemed like a good copy of the White House, where a staff of maids and governesses skated silently over the magnificent parquet floors.

It smelled of wax and pastries, while our house stank of onions.

As if that weren't enough, the little "master" also played the violin.

I instinctively felt that he really belonged to another category. Those parents, that wonderful-smelling house, those elegant servants. Well! Faced with this, it's better to be the son of the watermelon vendor in Piazza San Marco than to be that sort of mediocrity which my family and I were.

At that time, I was unaware of the term "petty bourgeois," but I was deeply and humiliatingly conscious of inferiority. In other words, I felt like a worm.

What didn't make sense, though, was the incredible affection that Alvise's mother, that divine, angelic lady, showed toward mine.

And yet, those two completely different women embraced each other tearfully when they first met on the beach, and went on hugging and smiling for hours as they talked affectionately, sitting on two bamboo chairs in the splendid garden of the "Ombreggiata."

The explanation goes back to my grandmother's tits.

My grandmother Caterina was a hefty country girl, known as "Big Caterina of the Blooming Hills," precisely because her tits were renowned for being the most abundant in the entire region of Treblinka.

Because of this attribute, my grandmother was chosen by Count Kovalensky as a wet nurse for his beloved firstborn—a choice which enabled Caterina's daughter and the count's daughter to grow up like sisters, up to the age of fourteen.

That's when the little countess was sent off to faraway Italy, to a boarding school in Florence, where a few years later she came out on the arm of the Count Ottolenghi Portaleoni, of a noble and Jewish Ferrara family, while my mother had to wait for Mr. Coleman Hassalonn Towermann, in other words, Papa, a Polish-American whose bride she became, and they sailed toward dear old New York.

These milk-sisters therefore, our mothers, were crazy about each other. It was obvious. Whereas I can't really understand why my dear mamma didn't commit suicide, faced with that milk-sister who was a sort of fairy, a nymph, a kind of goddess. But Mamma didn't have any complexes . . . as I did with Alvise.

I remember that princely Villa Ombreggiata like a nightmare—that large salon, through whose windows you could see the marvelous garden where our two mothers, the milk-sisters, kept chattering away. Alvise is playing the violin.

How does he play it? Come on! Wonderfully!

The virtuosity of his playing is extremely irritating to me. As I listened, I picked my nose. A bit later, I discover an incredible painting on the wall behind him.

There's the head of this guy on a silver platter, cut off from the body and ready to be served like a dish of calf's head. A scene that fascinates me. And there's a girl, full of colored veils and jewels, who is dancing.

Alvise, handsome, blond, poet and violinist, draws

the last note with the bow. He opens his eyes, which have been half-shut in rapture over the music, and follows my gaze to the painting.

"Do you like John, the prophet?"

"Who?"

"John, the prophet," Alvise says. "Salome dances in front of King Herod because she wants the head of John the Baptist. And, in fact, Herod gives it to her. It's Salome's dance. It's in the Holy Scriptures. Salome and her Dance of the Seven Veils."

I immediately have a clear idea of women.

"What a bitch! What does that bitch of a bitch have against John?"

"Well, I think it's because he's pure. Because he's a saint. He's John the Baptist, the prophet. And God talks with him . . . But not with her! God doesn't talk with Salome. It's a Palma . . ."

And he points to the painting with his bow. I shake my head.

"Hold on . . . Hold on. What's a palm tree got to do with this guy?" Alvise smiles kindly.

"Oh, no. Sorry. Palma the Elder has nothing to do with the story of Salome and the Baptist. He's a painter. He's the one who made the picture."

And he smiles. That cute, sweet tone really gets to me. All right. Sure. I don't study and I even get bad grades in school, but I bet that nobody knows this old painter guy.

I feel like asking Pa. But I suddenly realize that Pa doesn't know anything about this old guy with the palm tree. Damn, this little smartass is really getting on my nerves. Oh, well. With a diplomacy that surprises even me, I let the matter drop.

I go back to talking about the dancing bitch in the painting.

"Well, anyway, I think that Salome is just jealous. Yeah, just like old Betsy, the shopping-bag lady. You know, Betsy's so jealous that she stands outside the Plaza Hotel and yells to the rich people getting into their limousines, 'Get cancer and drop dead, you bastards!' Hey, you know New York, don't you?"

Alvise smiles, courteously and modestly.

"No."

Great! I like that! Finally, a point in my favor. I proudly raise my head.

"Well, I do."

I look at the painting again. It's like a scene out of a movie.

"Nice stuff! It's like a scene out of a movie."

"Oh, it's an old family painting. You must have family paintings too, don't you?"

He's only trying to be nice, but he really gets to me.

"Nope! We've only got diamonds in our house."

Haughtily turning up my big nose, I tell him.

"Pa buys and sells them, see? And that's why we're here. Pa says that with all the Jews running out of Germany, you can do good business."

I go on loudly, not realizing that the two mothers are coming back into the house.

"Yeah, because Papa says that when the Jews run away from Hitler, they hide diamonds up their bums, 'cause it's sure money . . . in a safe place! And then they sell them for good prices, 'cause they need the dollars. The only problem is that they have to be washed, right?"

And I begin to laugh wildly, as Alvise stares at me in astonishment.

Yeah, sure, I must seem horribly vulgar to him. And I am, but I tell the truth. I mean, Christ! The truth is vulgar, and horrible, right? And also unfair. Because I get a terrific smack across the face!

My mother has just heard the last part of what I was saying, and gives me a monstrous slap to keep me quiet.

"What in the world are you saying, Sammy? Stop it this instant!"

"But if Papa said it . . ."

Mamma gives me another stinging smack. The sympathy and complicity in Alvise's eyes—that blond, fondled and petted little violinist—just makes things worse. I'm the unhappiest child in the world.

Actually, it was a moment of happiness. Except that I didn't know it. Even Alvise and the parents weren't really aware of what was going on, there in Venice at the end of that summer. Venice, full of high officials in uniform, movie stars in bathing suits and elegant Germans flitting around in motor boats.

The mothers did feel a certain apprehension. Europe was quite tense because of that hysterical man with the little mustache. In short, war was feared. So, to ease their fears and homesickness, both mammas had a brilliant idea. As if to sanction the bizarre scheme of fate that had made them meet again, in that particular summer, and right here in Venice.

And, in fact, right in the garden of the Villa Ombreggiata. Alvise's mother, that beautiful goddess, had a brainstorm.

"You know what we'll do? We'll go to Poland and see Mamma Caterina. The European situation is so unstable. And that Hitler has a nasty temper. Let's go back to our native land before he does something crazy. And Sammy and Alvise will be able to see Poland and meet Mamma Caterina. She'll be so happy. Let's leave immediately."

A brilliant idea! Everyone was enthusiastic about it. Fathers, mothers and us kids.

"Yes. Great. Let's leave immediately."

What is known as having a sense of timing . . . exceptional timing. It was worse than a date.

We arrived in Treblinka almost at the same time as the Panzer Division. Hitler wasn't playing around. They stopped us. And they packed us up like sardines in one of the first sealed SS trains. We probably inaugurated it. And the rest of the vacation continued courtesy of the Third Reich. But in another climate altogether.

Today, thinking back on it, there are certain parts of New York that are so overcrowded with the children and grandchildren of Israel that one might just believe that little joke about the German repentance machine, where you stick a bar of soap in one end and a Jew pops out on the other side.

But not back then! We had no idea what the camps were all about.

We only got a small glimpse of that enormous and

abominable horror. Our own little piece of horror merely seemed like a sort of nightmare—of cold, of hunger, of death.

For many years after that, and still now, when there is a garden party and I hear someone say: "I'm starved," or "It's freezing out," I shiver. Those who haven't fought tooth and nail, fingers in eyes and kicks below the belt, for a dirty potato peel, those who haven't sunk their feet into the guts of a horse disemboweled by a bomb, to avoid freezing to death, don't know the real meaning of these words.

The last human memory was the strange sound of hundreds of children's voices calling out "Mamma" as they were being divided into the big ones and the little ones. After which, an Olympic game of resistance and ability began, which didn't leave much time for sentimentality.

The only game permitted us kids was fooling the most severe of all the nurses. Oh, that fräulein had many wonderful names: the Grim Reaper, the Exterminating Angel, Azrael, Thanatos—or, in the more Asian version, Kali with her Danse Macabre. It was that old bitch, Death, who came to reap the fields of our defenseless childhood; and for us, the game was to screw her in some way. In other words, it was a matter of staying alive.

And warding off Death was anything but easy in that place, given the fact that, with their super-organized cultural-scientific preparation, the SS had programmed everything in order to execute mass death like an assembly line. They had a high productivity quota, and did their best not to bring it down, thanks to their highly specialized personnel.

During those years we spent inside that place so lovingly prepared by the prize firm "Hitler und Himmler," the problem in reality was not dying, which on the contrary had its good points, and let's say easy ones too. The real problem was living, an extremely difficult task.

The nice part of our stay there was that, at sunset, we were filled with longing, smelling the aroma of roast meat which wafted over from the adult section. We were sure that the administration was passing out meat to the adults. Only after many years did we discover the horrible truth about those roasts. And still today, roasts are banned from my menu.

Naturally, during all this time, Alvise was like a guardian angel to me. According to the programs suggested between the lines of *Mein Kampf*, the protective concept of "Mamma" was rapidly substituted with *kapòs*, armed with whips and German shepherds.

In their essential language, they rapidly invented an esperanto, which we kids immediately comprehended. The notions contained in those orders were few and concise. We would have to go without food, stand for hours on end in the courtyard, get whipped and be sent into "transport," a word with a very simple meaning: You were *transported* from "here" to the "beyond."

It's useless to get caught up in details.

It's history that everybody knows, right? And according to some serious historians, not even one of the worst that mankind has produced.

As if the rest of the program weren't enough, one fine day the bombings began. Well, you won't believe it, but for us it was a party.

You had to be there to see us, in the livid light of the bombs, us little prisoners, in groups, running around and scrambling over holes and corpses.

Yes, why deny it, it was a real party. Especially when some blessed lynx-eyed Yankee struck Hilde the Kapò dead-center.

Bull's eye! We all ran up and began circling around that cow. Bitch of a bitch. Daughter of a bitch. Granddaughter of a bitch. I can still remember her enormous white buttocks.

It's difficult to explain: It's not as though we were impelled by morbid or erotic motives, but the first thing that was done, in those cases, was to undress the corpse, or what remained of it.

Sure, then there was a great deal of pilfering, rummaging and looting. We had a black market. And with that damn cold, a pair of woolen underpants were enough to get you half a loaf of bread. But besides the useful, there was also the pleasurable.

I'm talking about that famous night. When that sharpshooting Yankee hit "Big Tushy Hilde" the Kapò dead-center. Oh, yes! Yes! A real party. It would take Freud's pen, along with that of de Sade, to properly recount that party.

We snuck into the barracks and closed ourselves in while the bombings continued outside.

I remember the sounds of whispering and the great agitation, in the shadows of the barracks.

Everyone was running. Even the smallest ones who

looked like cadavers got up their strength to join the group. And everything took place in a silence full of whispers. An older child stood guard by the door.

Everything went well until Alvise came along.

That's right, I forgot to mention that during our little bombardment-orgy, that ball-breaking Alvise wasn't there. Who knows where he went under the bombs. I bet to help some blind SS faggot cross the street. Or probably to talk to the birds, to persuade them to forgive their flying-fortress brothers. Anyway, you can bet that he did some good deeds, worthy of a little Saint Francis.

From the moment he opened the barracks door, he knew what was going on. He froze on the threshold, and sniffed the air.

"What's going on? What are you doing?"

He whispered, troubled. Fearing the worst, he ran toward the group that was hovering about the stove. And it *was* the worst. Something was roasting that sent delicious aromas around everywhere.

"But . . ."

Alvise, with two bulging eyes, grabbed me just when, with my mouth open, I was about to bite into a piece of roasted meat. He seized my hand, and I naïvely held out the piece of meat to him.

"Taste this roast, taste how good it is. And to think she was so mean."

He immediately realized the atrocious truth. But he had trouble believing it. He almost couldn't talk.

"What are you eating?"

"The sergeant's ass. You know, the *kapò*. Big Tushy Hilde."

In fact, the roast consisted of one large buttock. The other one had already been carved, like a roast beef, and all the children were eating, happy and satisfied.

I don't know who said that revenge is a dish that is eaten cold. Maybe it was hunger, but I assure you that the *kapò* was excellent, even hot and cooked as she was.

With the simple and clear ideas of childhood, we children were overjoyed. But that implacable pain in the ass, Alvise, was overcome with horror, and started screaming:

"No! No . . . "

And he grabbed me by the arm and dragged me away with all his might, completely horrified. Goddammit! The one time we could eat . . . I tried to resist.

"But why? It's good! Wait . . . "

Nothing doing! He ruined the party for me.

He told me that what we were doing was horrible. He dragged me outside, under the bombs, despite my screams.

One big pain in the ass. He didn't have any peace until he made me feel guilty.

Outside, the bombing continued.

The camp was devastated and we were fighting in the glare of the bombs and fire.

"No . . . I'm not bad. She was the one who was bad. They are bad."

"Yes. But this doesn't mean you have to become like them. You're also a bloodthirsty beast."

"She was shit! A disgusting, stinking old bitch! And we did well . . ."

I dug my heels into the ground with all my might.

"Let me go back. I'm hungry. The one time we can eat something, dammit!"

But Alvise was like a madman. Really overdoing it.

"No . . . No! Come on! Let's go toward the vegetable gardens. Maybe we'll find a potato or something. So then you won't think about that horrible thing anymore."

He dragged me through the darkness until a bomb fell right near us.

We dropped to the ground just in time. Christ, what a blast!

When we got up, we found a smoking crater in front of us.

The bomb fell on the barbed-wire area. The high-tension wire made a sudden flash.

By that livid light, we saw a great gash in the fence. Alvise looked beyond into the darkness that followed the flash. For a moment, there was only silence. Darkness and silence.

"Sam . . . Did you see?"

"Shit! What a hole!"

The bombs, blasts and flashes began again. Alvise had a strange expression on his face.

"Could it be a sign from heaven? Do you think you can do it? Shall we try?"

And cocking his head, he made a sign to escape.

I looked at him, eyes wide open. He was really out of his mind.

"You're out of your mind. They'll catch us and feed us to the dogs. I'm scared. . . . No way!"

Alvise was excited. He looked at me with apprehension, aware of his responsibilities.

"How can I leave you here? You're too little for this place!"

I didn't like that look of his. I tried to sound casual.

"It's all right. Don't worry. I'll manage."

"No. It's either now or never again! Come on!"

He grabbed my hand and dragged me in the dark, toward the large hole outside the camp.

Sure, without him I would have never had the courage to escape from that hell, and certainly, by now, I would be a fertile lump of German soil. But when we found ourselves in the dark, at night, in that deadly cold, and heard the dogs barking in the distance, I began to conceive an even greater hatred for Alvise. Greater than . . .

I mean, there are cracks that become crevices, and then abysses . . . Damn! If he was better than me, and felt like playing the hero, what the hell did I have to do with it?

He made me walk through an icy stream so we wouldn't leave a trail. We walked till dawn. It was cold . . . so cold . . .

I know. Sure, he was always right, damn him.

But I can assure you that it was very, very irritating!

What's more, he remembered all the stories about the Indians. He was incredible. He knew how to tell the direction of the wind by licking his finger and holding it out in the air. At first, I hoped he'd go wrong. He said south, and who could prove the contrary? But dammitall, it did turn out to be south.

He knew we had to cover up our doody. He knew how to read the clouds and smell a storm. He even knew how to carry me on his shoulders when I couldn't walk anymore.

He knew how to identify the nest of I don't know what kind of bird. He knew how to find its eggs, which he then made me eat.

In short, it was like going around with a platoon of young explorers or those damn Boy Scouts. He was like Crazy Horse's wise cousin. Davy Crockett was an amateur next to Alvise.

So, from the top of a tree he located the exact position of a railway line, which he discovered earlier by putting his ear to the ground. Then he threw me from a tree branch onto a moving, whistling train. It was enough to break both legs and end up with us crushed under the wheels.

Alvise was definitely lucky and protected. It seemed as if there were an enormous hand over his head, sheltering him from danger. He had some kind of supernatural "connection." We didn't get hurt, and we took shelter inside a railway car. We hid inside two mail sacks in a car full of postal material. Only our heads stuck out. In there, with the clickety-clack of the wheels and my fear, I began to feel very sleepy. Hah! Fat chance! My ballbreaking guardian angel Alvise began to shake me.

"Wake up, Sammy! You have to wake up."

"Oh, Christ . . . When we can eat, you don't let me eat, when we can sleep, you won't let me sleep! . . . What a pain in the ass!"

"You're little, Sammy. You can't understand. Come on . . . Take off your clothes."

Like a little mother, Alvise undressed me as I went on

yawning and dozing. He took off my camp rags and substituted for them an imaginative outfit made out of the mail sacks.

"We can't go around Germany in our camp uniforms. This way, we'll only look like two beggars. Then there's something else we have to do. . . ."

He pulled out my skinny little arm. On the inside of my wrist were inscribed the indelible numbers of the prison camp, a fatal tatoo.

"And now we have to make these disappear. And there's only one way to do it. . . ."

He rummaged through the train car and found an old lamp. He broke it. He took one of the glass shards. He made a little fire out of some envelopes from the postal sacks, with a match he had miraculously saved in his pocket. He burned the remains of our uniforms, to avoid leaving tracks. Then he disinfected the piece of glass.

I watched his movements with indifference.

"Hey . . . watcha doin'?"

Alvise smiled at me sweetly.

"Here, watch. We only have to scrape a bit here . . . like this . . ."

As he spoke, he scraped at the indelible numbers on his wrist, bearing the pain heroically.

"So that it bleeds a little bit, and then a scab will form and hide the numbers. There . . . like that. Come on . . . You do it too."

I was terrified.

"But doesn't it hurt?"

"No, not really. Just a little bit."

I faltered and then took the piece of glass. I began to

graze my toothpicklike arm with extreme care, grumbling like a cranky old man.

"What a pain in the ass. Ooooh . . . Owwww . . ."

A sudden braking of the train accomplished the work I hadn't the courage to complete. I fell forward and cut my arm with the piece of glass. I screamed like a pig.

"Owwwwwwwwww! Owwwwwwww!"

Alvise threw himself on top of me and covered my mouth with his hand. The train was just coming into a station.

"Ssssh . . . Otherwise they'll find us. Disinfect yourself with the ashes. You did a good job! Quick . . ."

He looked out.

"Let's jump here."

I looked at him as if he were crazy.

"But the train's moving."

"Yes . . . but slowly. Out . . . now's the time . . ."

"No. No . . . I'm not gonna jump. I'm not . . ."

Alvise gave me an affectionate shove.

"Come on . . . The station's coming up."

"No. I said noooooo . . ."

Alvise gave me a strong but affectionate kick that sent me flying out of the car. Then he flung himself down along the slope after me.

I remember that it was still nighttime, and the German countryside was cold and hard as we rolled down the side of the track. The train passed. I was furious because I'd hurt my knee.

And I had even more of a grudge against Alvise. But a few seconds later, the train leapt up in the air. Hit by the first bomb of another bombardment.

Alvise, as always, had been right.

And he was also right when he decided that we should go into the city during the bombardment.

He was right again, later on, while we were walking amid the rubble, when he decided that we should pass as victims of the bombardment, so that we could find something to eat. Naturally, we had to look like Germans.

Needless to say, he spoke German fluently, and I would pretend I was mute from shock. But there was one inconvenience. . . .

I realized it later, when we were in a crumbling cellar. I noticed Alvise staring at me. At this point, I was distrustful and very suspicious. I knew that there was always trouble behind that intense gaze of his.

"What is it? Why ya lookin' at me like that? Whatsamatter? Huh?"

Alvise shook his head.

"That nose . . ."

I touched my nose, puzzled.

"What is it? What's the matter with my nose? Why?"

"Well, it's a sort of factory trademark. I mean, if they look at your profile, they'll realize immediately that we're Jews . . . and they'll send us back to the camps. . . ."

"There, I knew it. They'll feed us to the dogs, damn you. I knew it! Couldn't you have thought about it before? Whatta we do now?"

"Sssssh."

Flashlight beams ripped through the darkness. Soldiers' voices.

I jumped up in terror and attempted to flee, but Alvise suddenly tripped me and I fell to the ground, crushing my big nose. I never knew whether it was an accident or a strategic attack on Alvise's part. It hurt like hell. Alvise came over to check me out, and taking advantage of my shock, rapidly released a terrible punch on my aching big nose. Treacherous blow—terrible pain.

I screamed. I felt something warm dripping in my mouth.

After throwing dirt and debris over both of us, Alvise immediately fell to the ground and also began screaming. Naturally, in German. He cried for help, for Mamma, and other things like that, which made rescue come instantaneously.

Yeah, he was right again, dammitall. The blood gushing from my big swollen nose not only helped us in not being recognized as Jews, but also in being affectionately picked up, cared for, and most important, fed, like well-deserving citizens, war victims, victims of those s.o.b. Yankee bombers, little heroes of the Third Reich's internal front.

We recovered in a nice German hospital.

They stuck an enormous bandage on my nose. They put us among a sea of wounded and stitched children, and shoved bowls of thick, steaming soup in our hands.

A few days later, Alvise, the infallible boy-wonder, decided it was time to split, out of general prudence and also on account of a certain something . . .

We happened to be in the hospital bathroom with the other children. We were all standing under the steaming showers, and naturally we were all naked. Alvise looked down below my round belly, and suddenly noticed something that concerned the both of our, how can I put it, wee-wees, *putzes*, penises, peckers, you know, *schlongs!*

Vigorously, German nuns and nurses were taking turns scrubbing and lathering the children amid the steam. Alvise, alarmed, made a sign that I didn't understand, and stared at me right *there.*

Well, it was something quite exceptional. I don't know whether I already mentioned it or not, but I am super-endowed. Even as a child. My poor papa used to tell me that the object which made me a little man was an orangutan, a leopard, a roaring jaguar, of imposing proportions. Oh, he was so proud of those proportions! And since I was little, it made me feel like a sort of super-male, a kind of chosen being.

That's why I, although quite innocent, felt suspicious when Alvise looked at me right there. At first, I thought it was jealousy, or something worse. But it wasn't an erotic stare. As usual, he was right: We were circumcised! That's what he was looking at.

If we didn't get out of there fast, they would have discovered that we were circumcised. And then we would have become food for the starving camp dogs.

Alvise was wonderful. Damn him . . .

First of all, he grabbed me and, with little regard for my delicate, erogenous perpendicular appendage-captain's honor zone, which later would become the center of production, pleasure and posterity, and which was already, despite its very young age, an article of considerable grandeur, although fragile and sensitive, began to rub soap over it vigorously, as if he were a washerwoman!

The nasty soap of those terrible hospitals, in those terrible years, with those terrible stories—in the camps it was said to be made out of the fat of us Jews, but I don't believe it, I think that was just bullshit! Because, in the camps, very little fat was left on the Jews, and the expense wouldn't have been worth the undertaking. It was a sort of brown brick. When you scrubbed it over your body, it shredded your skin like sandpaper. There wasn't any fat in it at all, and as for the suds, you really had to scrub and scrub to get any out. All this vigorous scrubbing over the "erogenous zone" was also quite embarrassing. Alvise really made me suffer a lot.

The pain exceeded my shyness and complexes. Oh, yes! There we were, naked under the steamy showers. Those are delicate parts that, when you're little and alone, you might touch with an idle hand, or at most, might be touched by mammas, affectionate servant girls, aunts, grandmothers, governesses, wet nurses. But if anybody else comes near, these delicate parts should be defended with might and main, right? But what could anyone defend from that screwball? The only good side to all of this was that the violence of Alvise's vigorous and determined lathering did keep the complexes and shyness under control.

There was also his hand on my mouth. Yes. Because Alvise was lathering me with one hand, and with the other he covered my mouth, to prevent me from screaming.

With all that scrubbing, he finally did manage to make some little brown suds come out of the brown brick, and with those suds he managed to hide my *petite-*

chapelle-prépuce. After he finished with mine, he worked on his.

With a few suds and a lot of luck, we managed to pass under the probing eyes of the shower sector's nurse, who in fact resembled Big Tushy Hilde the Kapò.

Sure. Everything went okay then, but now it was time to split, and quickly. Alvise conceived a diabolical plan: Operation "Blond Baby-Doll."

All said and done, with the violence typical of a man of action, which I had often found in him, he grabbed me by the hand in the midst of all the confusion—the vapors of the showers, the crying babies, the wounded children, the stretcher-bearers, the nurses, all in the deafening din of a child's purgatory—and dragged me to the dressing rooms. We went up to a wooden door marked "F"—for females.

He snuck in and grabbed some little dresses, bonnets and shoes, and wrapped them all up in a sheet. Then we went down a rickety staircase that stank of phenol acid.

We made a speedy "hit and run" raid of the emergency room, where Alvise stole a small bottle of hydrogen peroxide.

It must have been a section of the hospital connected with first aid and with the emergency organization for bombardments. When the city was bombed, they received cartloads of wounded, mutilated bodies, and even corpses.

Behind a gate was a series of familiar constructions. They were, in fact, the morgue and the crematorium.

So, going in there, for me, was a bit like visiting my

old Aunt Agatha. But when it was time for action, Alvise didn't get lost in details.

He dragged me into a sort of broom closet, and indifferent to my protests, began to busy himself with me and with my head.

"Ooooooh . . . Ooooh . . . Why? Whattaya doin' to me?"

"We have to get out of here."

"I don't wanna go away. They feed us here."

"Come on, don't be cranky. After the shower, at the medical checkup, they would have seen that we're circumcised."

"Okay, okay . . . but what is it, after all? Even Papa used to talk about it all the time, about circumcision. Does it have to do with jerking off?"

"Oh, come on, stupid, you don't know what circumcision is? It's when they cut off your foreskin. An ancient religious ritual that probably originated from an archaic nature cult—at least that's what my father told me. It's the phase of the cult that follows the one where human sacrifices were made in honor of the god of procreation. The ancient doctrine tells us that God had the ritual imposed directly on Adam, who circumcised himself at the age of ninety-nine."

"Damn! Ninety-nine years old! What the hell coulda been left to circumcise on that poor sausage? . . . probably just a cobweb."

Well . . . all right. Overlook my vulgar reply. I willingly repeat Alvise's explanation, not only to stimulate in the reader a hatred for the boy-wonder's irritating and presumptuous tone, but also because of another consideration. I happen to have the utmost respect for my coreligionists. I've been told that in the whole world, there aren't more than ten million of us. I think there have to be more than that, but woe to anyone who argues against the statistics. The system would fall to pieces. Anyway, I was saying, I think it's only fair that less-informed readers also have the right to more precise information on circumcision.

In any case, while Alvise was giving me this lesson, he was also working on my head with the hydrogen peroxide and busying himself with the clothes he'd stolen from the girls' dressing room.

Then, the usual air attack took place. The town was an important railway junction. The bombs kept coming.

The doors of the hospital blew open, and we slipped out amid the confusion, and the wagons and cars bringing in the wounded and the dead.

The most garish item in the clothes stolen from the girls' dressing room—a horrible little skirt covered with cherries and birds—dangled awkwardly around the skinny, bony hips of a starving little Jewish boy. Myself.

I only had a quick glimpse of my reflection in a piece of broken glass on the street.

Alvise dragged me away.

He wouldn't even think of giving me enough time to check myself out.

So that's how I found myself in a German railway station, dressed like a little girl, hand in hand with Alvise.

My hair, which was just beginning to grow back on

my bald head, had been bleached blond, along with my eyebrows, from the hydrogen peroxide.

The big nose was still under the bandage. I was wearing the horrible skirt with the cherries and birds, a little Dutch blouse and even a ruffled bonnet.

I was a hideous little girl. I hated Alvise with a wild passion.

He was calm as he dragged me by the hand. He went to ask a railway official some information in German, who gave it to him, looking at me with pity. Even a little girl has the right to some limits in her being ugly. I surpassed them all.

I had a humiliating experience of transvestitism. I scratched myself all over, suffering from a thousand complexes—*I*, who had never had any before, I got all of them, damn him. A little Jewish boy, proud of his generous nose and the promising beast tucked in his pants, now found himself stuck in a little German baby-doll skirt, covered with cherries and birds. I had the urge to pull up my petticoats and show everyone the reality of the situation. But the SS were passing back and forth with their sheepdogs.

So, despite my complexes and hatred, I realized that Alvise, once again, was right.

He pissed me off, dressed like that, in boy's clothing, and also because he had naturally blond hair, with sky-blue eyes and a stupid, stupid nose. Yeah, his nose . . . If you go by geometric correlations, evaluating the size of his nose, his "beast" must not have been such a big deal.

As I went on contemplating the likely measurements

of our masculinity, perfect Alvise, the boy-wonder, was looking for a way to cross the frontier.

It was a huge railway station, full of tracks, trains, bombardments, SS, soldiers, and thank God, a lot of confusion. We found a long freight car on a side track, and a car that wasn't sealed. I don't know how Alvise knew it was heading for France. We slipped inside like mice.

I found myself in a sea of horns and large, moist eyes that stared at me. For a moment, I was afraid. But there was something reassuring in the smell of all those cows, and their warmth. So, why not? Actually, they weren't bad as traveling companions.

For a moment, I almost felt happy, despite everything, when the train set off on her departure to France.

For France and her great cuisine . . . Yes, I must confess, it must have been hunger, but in my little undernourished head, the word "France" unleashed a conditioned reflex, and instead of thinking of Paris, or *la Cité des Lumières,* or Napoleon or *la Pucelle d'Orléans,* I thought exclusively and passionately of onion soup, *soupe aux oignons* as the French call it.

What Italian said "The shortest distance between two points is the arabesque"? Well, it may be an ironic line, but for us, if it wasn't the shortest, it certainly was the safest. We made arabesques throughout Germany, Austria, Bavaria, the Ruhr, Prussia and Central Europe.

We were often forced to change our means of transportation. We even had to leave that cattle car bound for France because of my unsuccessful attempt to attach myself to a teat full of milk, but I hadn't calculated the little lamb's nasty character, nor the degree of neurosis in cows while they are traveling. Plus, they must have been in full menopause. They woke Alvise up. Sure, I had attempted the conquest of the teat in one of those rare moments when my royal pain in the ass, super-ball-busting friend and guardian angel was taking a nap. Who knows why cows get so pissed off. They joined together in a sort of collective hysterical attack, which forced us . . . that is, which forced Alvise to kick me out of the train in the middle of the night.

Anyway, as I was saying, after that first cattle car, we tried every possible and imaginable means of transportation.

A bus with an outside platform . . . hay carts . . . bicycles . . . cars, wagons . . . Anyway, it took us two whole months to cross that damn border. And we crossed it in a canoe. Right. Worse than in a B-western. It's nice to read adventure stories about traveling and hunting when you're snuggled in a nice warm bed, after a good meal, just before your mother kisses you good night. But it's something else to find yourself being tossed about by violent waves in a river of menacing whirlpools, to cross the border in a sort of carnival canoe, stolen from a bombed-out storehouse in an amusement park by Alvise. It was terrifying, also because at night the river was black and icy, and while Alvise was rowing with a paddle, I had to empty the water out with a little can, keeping up a frantic rhythm so we wouldn't sink. A nightmare, one of many. Well, we finally arrived in France. Wet, but we made it!

Then we found out it was just the same as Germany
—SS, police dogs and terror. . . .

We found ourselves in a little French town, which
was charming, but also a bit melancholy. Alvise held my
hand as always, and dragged me through the streets.

We stopped at a corner to catch our breath, and something struck me.

A theater poster pasted on the wall.

Salome dancing with her seven veils, the decapitated
prophet and Herod, all sketchily painted.

"Salome. Remember, Sammy? . . . The painting in the
Villa Ombreggiata?" Alvise whispered to me.

I felt the wing of destiny grazing us, and I wanted to
cry. The nice lady who was dancing in the theatrical
poster had nothing in common with her colleague in the
Venetian painting, but at that moment, I felt that the
image would stick with me forever. Salome, who asked
and obtained, by way of her graces, the head of the
enemy. I knew that in some strange, serious and strategic
way this image would become part of me, of my life, and
my destiny, like my flesh and my heart . . . like that
roasted buttock belonging to Big Tushy Hilde.

Alvise, on the other hand, did not abandon himself to
stupid sentimentality. Instead, he immediately realized
how he could take advantage of the situation.

He revealed an unexpected knowledge about theatrical habits. And the fact that he spoke French like a Parisian isn't even worth bringing up.

Well, I don't know how he found out about the current salaries for daily walk-on parts, but the fact is that

he offered the company two walk-on page boys for half the price of the regular wages. At that time, in the French provinces, unions were as scarce as francs. Result: We found ourselves on the stage of the "Théâtre Municipale."

"I don't love your flowing tresses. It's your mouth I want to kiss, oh, Jochanaan! I want to kiss your mouth, oh, Jochanaan! It's like a beautiful purple ribbon circling an ivory tower. It's like a pomegranate split down the middle by a blade of silver. Oh, Jochanaan!" Salome sang —a robust soprano wearing a lace-covered bodice, veils, jewels and little medals.

The opera, full of violin squeaks and hints of the Oriental splendors of the tetrarch's court, was performed as well as it possibly could have been under the circumstances. Black cloths and red smoke, silver tinsel and worthless Christmas tree ornaments . . . Anyway, to me it seemed like the court of the Sun King, compared to what I had seen lately.

I would even have enjoyed myself, if another injustice hadn't occurred. It set off a terrible itch in my nose. And, in fact, this was the beginning of a nervous tic which was to continue throughout my adolescence. Guess who started it? Beautiful, angelic Alvise was playing the role of the princess's personal page, dressed all in silver and sprawled on the steps of the throne. I was considered a Negro in every respect. I was covered with black shoe polish and had to hold an enormous, heavy pole which was topped by a big fan, plucked of all its feathers. And if that wasn't enough, I had to wave the thing up and down.

It was so heavy that I could hardly move it.

I was wiped out even during the audition, and during the rehearsals the impresario-director, seated in the empty stalls, kept yelling at me:

"*Le petit nègre! Agite le palmier! Plus érotique! Plus érotique!*"

Also, I was very confused, because there were two Salomes: the fat soprano with the varicose veins, and the other, who was short and skinny, wearing the same dress as the fat one, and who did the famous dance.

"Theatrical make-believe . . . special effects . . . stage magic! Shut up and wave that fan!" they all explained.

I was very distrustful.

And I continued observing the two Salomes. Each different from the other, but both completely unlike the Salome who danced in the painting back at the Ombreggiata. I swayed the flabellum and pondered these dissimilarities when everything was upset by a triple event. A false note, a nearby bomb, and a wailing air-raid siren.

Screams, darkness, confusion and explosions.

As usual, it was a bombardment.

Yeah, those of you in the younger generation, who have no idea what bombardments are really like, may be feeling bored and restless by their constant recurrence in this story. Damn him, he keeps bringing them up.

But that's what it was like back then. During that terrible period, which seems to have been quickly forgotten, the game of death and bombings was part of everyday life.

It was horrible, especially at night. I remember the screams. The panic. The darkness. Immediately, everything was interrupted. Eating, working, going to the bathroom, making love, chases between cops and robbers, murders, brain operations. The mournful, alarming and vaguely cinematographic sound of the siren cut everything short. As if by magic, the madness of death-with-a-bang took over.

The apocalypse never had such a sensational image of its own myth as it has in our century. I mean, the explosion of a bomb in the heart of a city, with consequent collapsing buildings and fires, piles of corpses and hideous mutilations, children blown to bits or buried alive, and other such things. This kind of catastrophe, in "Colossal Panavision with the Living Splendors of Technicolor," was performed with greater success by nature than by man. But in this lively twentieth century, technological industrialization has raised the level for these devastating catastrophes, obtaining considerable results. With the basic difference that nature only creates earthquakes every now and then, while the man-made bombardments in those years were a sad and constant habit, repeated in certain areas every night.

But let's go back to that siren and that alarm, in that French night at the theater, when the air raid abruptly stilled Salome's veils and their prophetic dance.

Everyone burst out of the theater, and we both rushed into the streets of the village while buildings collapsed, bombs exploded and fire destroyed what was left. There were "fireworks" over our heads that were more sensational than the ones they have on the Fourth of July over the Hudson River. We rushed into a packed cellar that resounded with the percussion of the bombs falling. You'd think that in such a situation people would remain motionless and ashen-faced, muttering desperate prayers and making vows and pacts with their patron saints:

"If you get me out of this hell alive, I promise I'll never smoke, drink or curse again." But in our air-raid shelter, a terrible fight broke out between the fat Salome and the skinny Salome. It was an old grudge over a dressing room.

I wonder how the argument ended. . . .

The theater was hit by a bomb, and so was the shelter where we hid with the company. But because Alvise had had an irritating intuition—thanks to his divine faculties —he had dragged me out of the shelter just before the door blew up.

That's how we managed to escape, and find ourselves in the open countryside.

We were thinking that things couldn't get any worse, when it suddenly began to rain. We took cover under the arch of a bridge. Fortunately, the blond page Alvise, the first-rate walk-on, had the right to a mantle with his costume. That sky-blue velvet mantle studded with semi-rusted gold stars became our blanket.

We woke up. There was an extremely anemic French sun. We felt like crap, with aches in our bones, as if we were ninety years old. We were damp and chilled. When we stretched ourselves out like cats, we whined with pain. What a shitty way to wake up! Well, anyway, there are a few good aspects to all these war stories of death, cold, danger and hunger, right? One is that you don't have to wash your ears. You can easily learn to get used to the nice, warm feeling of a dirty neck and black fingernails—they even have more flavor —and as for feet, well we won't go into that! Many years later, I even discovered that filth and foul odors are considered sexy by certain epicurean palates. Anyway, back then it was the good side of a bum's life to wake up in one's own cublike warmth. But forget it! Do you think that the flawless, fearless little knight, the boy-wonder, ex-Lord Fauntleroy and presently the little blond page, would ever compromise on the issue of clean ears? No way! We argued about washing every single morning of those long months. But every morning he managed to pull me toward the water, and he did so with the smugness of someone who knew he was right. Then he'd ask me afterward, "Isn't it true that now that you're clean, you feel better?" And every morning, I answered, "No!"

Even that first morning, Alvise, the super-clean guardian angel, dragged me to a little creek. Suddenly, we heard a deep, hollow laugh, and then a voice from the other side of the bridge:

"Hah, hah. 'I said of laughter, It is mad: and of mirth, What doeth it?' "

Alvise stopped. Under the bridge there was a very old man, lying beneath a cart. A great white beard and two shining eyes amid grimy rags. Alvise looked at him. Then, before I could make out what was going on, his loud, clear voice rang out.

" 'I sought in mine heart to give myself unto wine.' "

The old man sat up as if struck by lightning, and with a different, emotional voice he continued his strange monologue.

" 'Yet acquainting mine heart with wisdom.' "

Alvise responded immediately:

" 'And to lay hold on folly.' "

They laughed together. Alvise forgot about the freezing water. They approached and faced each other from opposite banks of the river.

"Who are you, that you can recite Ecclesiastes at your age?"

"And you, old man? You know that the SS are highly cultured. And if they hear you, they're not going to waste time asking for your papers. They'll shoot you first, and then check to see if you're circumcised."

"Yes, and what about you two? Dressed as if you came directly out of the Holy Scriptures."

His name was Solomon, but due to the abundance of Gestapo and SS around, he thought it would be more opportune to change his name. And what name did that great son of Israel choose? *Christian!* A lie for a lie, it's better to exaggerate, he said. At first, he even wanted to call himself Jesus Christ. But then he decided against it. After all, Christ was Jewish—and the SS weren't playing around.

He worked as a sort of gypsy. His cart was attached to a bicycle and he went around sharpening knives and scissors, and also repaired pots. He seemed to be some kind of knife-grinder, but in reality he was a chicken thief and a piper.

He was headed for Spain. He took us under his protection, so to speak, but as things turned out, we ended up protecting him. He had the kind of madness of a foolish yet brilliant genius, like a supreme gambler, and even though he was an expert in all the tricks of escape, he always seemed to be skating on the rim of an abyss . . . I think he liked the thrills.

It's useless to emphasize the fact that a frenzied passion sprang up between Solomon and Alvise. It became even more sublime when Solomon pulled out a harmonica from under his rags. He gave it to Alvise, and together they played duets on the pipe and harmonica.

They would gaze into each other's eyes like two sweethearts in front of a priest. And naturally, what they played had nothing to do with country polkas or little *Bal Musette*-type waltzes. Are you kidding?! Bach, Pergolesi, Purcell . . .

Like two madmen, they even played their music under the nose of the gendarmerie, and near the trucks of the German Gestapo. And right in front of the restaurants in little towns where the SS officials would be eating their meals.

And I would be in a cold sweat the whole time. They didn't realize that some rough sergeant might consider their heavenly, refined music as I did—a terrific pain in the ass—and thus, they risked arrest or worse.

Anyway, God bless music-loving officers and merry gendarmes. Thanks to them, we were able to make our way toward San Sebastián. When we finally arrived there, I was only able to see the village intermittently because I developed a new tic: I kept winking my eye fifty or sixty times in a row.

It first began during a prelude, a harmonica-pipe duet played by my two ineffable companions.

When we got to San Sebastián, Solomon threw himself down on his knees. He kissed the Spanish earth. A little while later, we discovered that he was mistaken. Further on, he kissed some more ground. He was mistaken once again. We were actually somewhere in the vicinity of Biarritz.

When we were sure it was Spain, Alvise put the harmonica to his mouth, and Solomon took out his pipe, and together they played a little sonata. Then they had a little drink. And thus, Solomon, playing and drinking, and breaking every tradition of a wise, aspiring prophet, ended up rip-roaring drunk.

Alvise and I dragged him through the little streets of the village, toward the country. He kept on yelling.

" 'A time to cast away stones, and a time to gather stones together. . . .' There is a sore evil which I have seen under the sun . . . The blindness of powerrrrrr! The great Shelomoh was known for his wealth and his knowledge, more than any other king on earth. Fill your stomach, Gilgamesh. Every day there will be a feast. Let there be joy night and day. The children of Abraham will sail their boats toward the Promised Land. There is a sweetness in the light and eyes see the sun happily. In the city of Cádiz there is a white door leading to the sky. He, whose name cannot be uttered, bless him, for He shall save us. Because we are the chosen people of the Lord. He whose name cannot be uttered shall save the chosen people."

He was really screaming like a madman, and Alvise tried to keep him away from the houses. When we got out into the fields, he tried to hide Solomon behind some bushes so that no one would hear him.

I helped him too, and hearing all this raving and singing of psalms and verses from the Old Testament, I was struck by certain things, especially that our people are the chosen ones of the Lord whose name cannot be uttered.

"The chosen people of the Lord?"

Solomon turned to me like a madman. He overwhelmed me with his great white beard, his fiery eyes and a terrible spray of one hundred and seventy-nine proof red wine. He literally burped in my face.

"Yes, we are the chosen people."

"Us Jews? Are you sure?"

"Of course I am. It says so in the Holy Scriptures!"

But recalling the camps and all that I'd seen throughout Europe, despite my young age, I refused to accept his statement. "There must have been a mistake in the translation. What a lot of bull! Or maybe the Germans just don't know how to read. The chosen people! We're drowning in shit!"

His eyes were blazing with a holy fire that even made me a bit afraid. He yelled:

"Silence! Blasphemous, faithless one . . ."

Fortunately, no one heard him in that emerging Spanish night. There was a merry little quarter-moon, young as the night. Maybe because it was Spain, but that quarter-moon peeping through the clouds looked exactly like the famous veiled moon in the song, which saw Rosita kissing Manuelo.

The next morning, the sun was shining and we could see all around us.

Spain!
It was incredible. We had finally made it.
Baroque cathedrals. Low, whitewashed houses. Flies. Misery. A woman with a mantilla in a black car!
A lace fan and a red rose. Tapping heels and the clicking of castanets. Ayayayayayayay!
Spain! *Olé!*
For the first time, I saw Alvise in difficulty. Intense physical joy. The tics disappeared. Finally, Alvise, with a lost expression in his eyes, couldn't understand a goddamn word of the language either. I even had precocious, accentuated manifestations of physical, sensual pleasure. It was the first time in a long time that I felt happy.

Happiness which began to dwindle away when I discovered how quickly Alvise was learning Spanish.

Solomon got along in all languages. He was international. He was the classic Wandering Jew. He knew that a Jew's best friend was flight, and he also knew that you had to adapt yourself to the customs of each country you passed through. When in Rome, do as the Romans do.

"Spain! It is time to draw closer to the Church, my beloved children. In Spain, the churches are obviously Catholic. We wouldn't be looked upon with suspicion in there. Beggars, bums, old drunks, the poor and the hungry are part of the furnishings of the Church. They are the 'tools of the trade.'"

Of course the atmosphere in a New York synagogue has nothing in common with that of a Spanish Catholic church.

The church we wound up in that day was dark and threatening.

A ceremony of some sort was taking place. There were about fifteen people gathered around the pulpit. A dark, severe man, strangely reminiscent of Torquemada, the cruelest priest of the Inquisition, stood before them. Solomon had told us about Torquemada when he gave us a little history lesson on Spanish Catholicism while crossing the border. Anyway, the priest's voice seemed to terrify his listeners.

We went inside quietly. Sneaking along the altars and the naves. We had a very precise plan of action. But I have to tell the truth: That dark chamber, full of mysterious lights and huge paintings of crucifixions, saints on clouds, flying angels and devils being driven back into the flames—hung imposingly above the altars, as if suspended over our heads—well, in short, it gave me the creeps. That church had the atmosphere of both a palace and a dungeon. And what if they found out who we really were, the enemy . . . in other words, those who put up the crosses? Or at least that's the way it seemed to me. You know, a guilty conscience doesn't need any proof, or historical facts, and certainly not bona fide, legal trials. A guilty conscience works on the indefinite. Well, back then I felt like the great, great, great grandchild of that soldier who drove the lance through that poor man hung on the cross. It took me many years to learn that it was not my ancestor at all, but a Roman soldier, who was guilty of the crime.

My anguished thoughts were suddenly interrupted.

A loud cry. It was Alvise. He had fallen to the floor in a convulsive fit.

Alvise, the little lord, with his blond grace and elegant refinement—damn him—had never lost his air of nobility despite all our terrible experiences. Therefore, the priest naturally mistook him for one of the tourists in the visiting group, a typical son of an overindulgent tourist father.

The priest ran over to him like a tender, loving little mother, while the whole group of believers stooped to fan, massage and caress the poor little blond boy.

Of course Alvise was great. He was born to act. His convulsions aroused everyone's pity.

They all busied themselves with him—the priest, the women and the men. Some wiped his face, some held him up and others waved handkerchiefs over him.

The whole scene mesmerized me. It was as if I were gazing into an abyss.

Our plan had been that I would act as the lookout, while Solomon attempted to open the alms box. The coins in that box were destined by right to the true chosen people—*us*, in other words. But instead of staying by my post, I wandered off to get a better look at the little blond angel's brazen face. Shortly afterward, I found myself on the steps of the altar. I was taken aback by the elaborate decor.

Those Catholics are really something! They're always beating their chests and asking for charity—and then take a look at that! Silver ornaments, jewels, bits of lace and precious embroidery. It was really luxurious stuff. There was even a bar.

I just couldn't resist. I got closer to the ritual decanters used for the mass. I looked at them, I sniffed at them and then I even tasted the consecrated wine. Not bad.

Then, holding the two decanters in my hands, I went over to where the group was standing, around Alvise. I held the decanters out to the priest. Well, can you believe it?! In all the confusion, he gave Alvise some of the consecrated wine to drink.

Everyone helped him. Some held Alvise's head, and others supported his shoulders.

A woman suddenly realized what we were giving him to drink and let out a scream.

"*Virgen de la cruz de los siete dolores! El vino consegrado! Padre!*"

The priest, upon discovering the holy decanter in his hand, realized what was going on. He stepped backward, his face green and horror-stricken.

"Sacrilege! Sacrilege!"

All hell broke loose. The priest instantly identified me as the sacrilegious sinner. He tried to grab hold of me.

I was terrified, and leapt like a cat.

I fell, spilling and breaking the holy decanters. Everyone went crazy and started running through the church wildly.

Alvise had stopped his convulsions and ran to help me.

The ferocious group ran after us, screaming threats. In the confusion, the sacristan ran into Solomon who, noticing the unfortunate turn of events, stopped trying to discreetly open the alms box, and thought it more expedient to tear the whole thing violently off the wall. He took the box and ran from the church, with the congregation following at his heels.

There was a painting of hell, showing the damned amid the flames. Well, compared to the hell in that church, the hell in the painting was ludicrous. Torquemada, the Inquisitor, pursued the infidels.

Sweet Jesus! I must confess that I even tried to make myself a little sandwich out of those little wafers the Catholics call "hosts." After all, bread and wine! Hell, I was hungry! Who can ever really imagine all that stuff about the body and blood of Christ? It's such a preposterous idea.

Solomon also managed to escape. We all ran madly down the narrow streets, chased by the priests and the group of tourists. By that time, after so many escapes, and despite the differences in age, Solomon, Alvise and I were off like Olympic runners at the starting line.

However, we were arrested one hour later.

But we managed to create such an infernal bedlam that Solomon was able to leap on a passing truck full of sheep. He hid among the terrorized animals. The truck disappeared toward the South. Lucky him!

While we were dragged away by the civil guard.

When in Rome, do as the Romans do.

Spain. *Dios. El Rey. La mujer.* The Inquisition. What a strange country. Alvise explained the situation to me quite clearly: torture, drawing and quartering, the rack and the auto-da-fé for heretics.

It was of vital importance that we reassure the authorities of the apolitical nature of our sacrilege.

Alvise told me that Spain was a country that had just gone through a very difficult period. He talked about the recent civil war, obviously from the Reds' point of view, because he condemned Franco—a certain general who was a friend of Hitler and Mussolini.

The bad guys had won, as often happens.

Alvise reassured me. We had nothing to be afraid of, because we were too young to be executed and too old to be taken in by some family. They would place us in an orphanage.

That's exactly what happened to us.

He was right again, as usual.

A week later, they put us on a rickety train and brought us to the orphanage. We found the old familiar setting—disgusting bowls of slop, hunger, iron discipline, shaved heads and other delightful customs, with a slight Spanish variation on the theme: We had our knuckles rapped with wooden rulers, we had to go to mass at five in the morning. It was a high mass—but for us it was a low mass. Low in the sense that we were forced to kneel on hard chick-peas as a penance, and we remained on our knees for the entire celebration of the mass. Some celebration.

Naturally, Alvise, who spoke for the both of us, didn't tell them that we were Jewish. Trusting people is fine, but distrusting them is even better. He had his own ideas about those severe, mysterious priests. They were the ones who scourged, quartered, tortured and burned the Jews. In short, according to the super-ball-breaker, the Spaniards were very imaginative, and it was better not to provoke them.

"It's important that they think we're Catholics like the others."

It wasn't difficult hiding ourselves in the long, gray line of orphans. Sooner or later, we'd get to the port. Sure, because I neglected to reveal a very important thing: We were now in Cádiz! And Cádiz just happened to be the port of hope for all European fugitives. You can imagine what it must have been like for the sons of Israel.

We had to wait a whole month before we got a chance to look around. Finally, we were given a day of leave.

Cádiz is a white, sunbathed town, with a port crowded with ships and boats of all sizes and colors. The streets were incredibly full of noisy, picturesque crowds.

Dark faces, dark hair, dark eyes, dark mustaches, dark eyebrows, white teeth, big women and a lot of confusion.

The only thing that showed any sign of order was *us*. An orderly line of poor little wretches who looked like miniature prisoners of war; little orphans and outcasts, wearing uniforms the color of rat droppings.

On the extraordinary day of our little "outing" to Cádiz, we went on a forced march through the gardens, up to the fortress, and then down through the ancient streets of the Old Quarter, then along the *avenidas* in the center of town, until we finally arrived at the port.

There was an indescribable amount of hustle and bustle. The sea was swarming with ships, boats, fishing crafts and seagulls. The pier was crowded with all sorts of things, and all sorts of people. There were porters, fishermen and women frying fish and shrimp over little fires. There were carts filled with lemons and ices, and peddlers selling sangría, jasmine water, candies and little dolls. Frenetic, happy, barefoot children were merrily yelling something about bullfights and toreadors.

Spanish gypsies were dancing, and the civil guards' tri-cornered hats were seen sailing over the sea of people. There were also crowds of people boarding the ships. There were so many ships—or at least, there seemed to me to be a lot.

We happened to be standing quite close to one of the ships. We could see the gangplank overflowing with emaciated, poverty-stricken emigrants. But there seemed to be a light glowing in their eyes. The hope of the voyage and the sea.

Of course! We knew only too well that ship meant life. The life that awaited them beyond the ocean.

They were like us: people who came from the most diverse, dispersed corners of this great, ancient, and to them, unfriendly continent of Europe—from the ghettos of Poland and Prussia, the French provinces, the Rumanian valleys, beautiful, sunny Italy and icy Lithuania. People who had lived through months, years, of terror, adventure, hunger, blackmail, humiliation, threats, evil tricks and sleepless nights. People who had seen their mothers and their children torn from them, and who had seen friends murdered, and relatives disappear. People who had heard others whispering terrible stories about incredible atrocities which couldn't be true, but were indeed true. People who had fear and death written on their faces. And yet, these same people now had hope in their eyes.

Without looking back, they boarded the ship. They didn't want to remember what they were leaving behind: their homes, their country, the camps and death.

The poor wretches were finally embarking for America.

Well! You can imagine what that ship meant for Alvise and me.

I fell into some sort of trance. My eyes were filled with tears as I stammered to myself:

"Gee, that ship's going to New York!"

Alvise, who stood by my side, tried to cheer me up.

"Sooner or later, a ship will take us there too, you'll see."

"Couldn't we try to take it sooner, instead of later? I can't take this anymore."

I sniffed with my big nose, and my hazel eyes were all swollen.

"Damn you. You're such hot stuff, think up something, why don't you? I wanna go home. Hopefully, Ma and Pa are already there."

Alvise looked at me.

"Calm down. Come on. You'll see, we'll find a way somehow."

We stood there looking at the long line of passengers with hungry eyes. Then our guardians began hurrying us away from the unusual gathering.

The crowd pushed us. The turmoil was growing.

All of a sudden, just as might happen in fairy tales, legends or real-life miracles, I heard the sound of a pipe. That sound made my heart leap and my stomach convulse with emotion.

Then I heard a voice.

" 'To everything there is a season, and a time to every purpose under the heaven: A time to be born, and a time to die. . . . A time to love, and a time to hate, a time of war, and a time of peace.' "

Alvise squeezed my arm as tightly as he could. I saw Solomon in the middle of the stream of the children of Abraham. He was pontificating like an ancient prophet, with his arms raised to the sky.

"Solomon! Solomon!"

I screamed wildly. It was our old dear friend, the Wandering Jew. He stood on the tips of his toes and looked over the sea of heads. Alvise picked me up and raised me above the people.

He recognized us.

It's difficult to recount what happened afterward, just as it is always difficult to recount a miracle. The old prophet, with those luminous eyes of his, managed to overwhelm the whole crowd. I don't know how he did it.

Finally, he came over to where we were standing. For a moment, he looked into our tear-filled eyes. His own eyes were radiating madness and faith. He looked down at our uniforms, and then at the ship leaving for New York. We made immediate contact—his wink was enough. Then he began to yell out his prophetic threats in a thunderous voice. I'm not sure, but I think he even faked an epileptic fit. He created a terrible amount of confusion: cries, screams, yells and a lot of people. The guards intervened. The priests were grabbed by their robes. The wave of revolt broke up the precarious order of the orphans' line. Even the guardians were pushed aside. Before anyone else could understand what was going on, Alvise and I were suddenly aboard the ship.

We were like frenzied little mice as we scampered between people's legs, under old peasants' skirts and up the gangplank. I don't think that any force on earth could have stopped us. The crowd simply swallowed us up.

We slipped inside a lifeboat on the side of the ship. Only there, through a crack in the rubberized canvas, did we dare to look out.

The uproar continued, thank God. I burst into tears.

I finally saw her again: the Statue of Liberty—that stately lady who illuminates us with her lamp. My eyes were veiled with tears as I gazed at her. Then I turned and glimpsed New York City in the foggy distance.

We couldn't get any closer to the city, because we were detained at Ellis Island. Six large warehouses, which had originally served as shelters for immigrants, were now being used as a juvenile refugee center.

Naturally, I had to erase all my childish hopes of ever finding Ma and Pa waiting for me, as if nothing had happened. There was no one there I could share my experiences with, because Alvise was implacably and constantly by my side. And all the other children were in similar situations.

Chocolates, sweets, milk, baths, hot showers and clean clothing. Oh, yeah . . . sure. Very comfortable. But a deep sense of alienation, of not belonging. It didn't even seem like I had come home. I also felt ashamed because my nice New York accent had become a terrible hodge-podge of foreign words and expressions. When I became fully aware of my new situation, I forgot the fact that I had finally been saved, and instead sank into a state of terrible melancholy. Alvise carried on like a guardian angel, naturally.

" 'Give me your tired, your poor, your huddled masses yearning to breathe free, the wretched refuse of your teeming shore. Send these, the homeless, tempest-tossed to me: I lift my lamp beside the golden door.' "

I glared at him through my tears. What the hell was he going on about?!

"Don't you see? Those are the verses written beneath the Statue of Liberty that welcome the poor immigrants! This is what makes America a great country."

Those noble words were really grating on my nerves. I had better let the melancholy mood pass; otherwise Alvise was capable of God knows what ball-breaking recitations.

I began to realize that there was a certain merriment around me. In fact, someone threw a ball at me and I caught it. You know how children are: You can tell them that they are poor, homeless orphans, but they don't give a damn, they just want to play.

A crowd of aspiring parents who stood behind the glass partitions were studying and considering us with their critical yet eager eyes. This filled us with such anguish that we screamed louder than ever, so we wouldn't have to think about it.

I wonder what it felt like in the ancient slave markets, or what it was like being part of the merchandise in a brothel. I mean, that feeling you have when you're waiting to be chosen is an awful thing to experience. Shit! What absolute shit! It was especially awful for those of

us who didn't have blond hair and sky-blue eyes. Right
—all the homeless children were Jewish, and all the aspiring parents were Jewish. But at that time, I didn't
know that the dream of many good grandsons of
Abraham was to have tall, blond children, especially in
New York, where the bosses are often tall and blond.
The same thing probably went for the Italians, Armeni-
ans, Puerto Ricans, Spaniards and Greeks. But with us
Jews, this obsession with blonds was really conspicuous.
Despite ancient rules and old family customs, many Hollywood stars and producers who were small, salty Jews
married six-foot-tall, blond girls of Lithuanian origin, to
improve the race. Hitler, Gary Cooper, Marilyn
Monroe, Candice Bergen—by the end of the century,
there were bound to be some changes.

Anyway, all the hopeful parents who had watched
us screaming, playing and making rude gestures and
noises finally made their decisions. It took all hundred
of us refugees about two weeks to realize that every
single one of them had chosen Alvise. Alvise, unlike us,
had been busy reading old books and magazines in a
little corner of the room. Of course they all wanted the
blond, beautiful, little Prince Charming, and they
didn't even know how good and intelligent he was.
They didn't even know he could play the violin. And
all those other marvelous things he could do. By choos-
ing Alvise, they had disregarded the rule that children
were to be adopted systematically, giving precedence to
the Americans, and the youngest ones, and so on. Alvise happened to be Italian and the eldest. The basic
problem was that Alvise didn't accept the idea of being

adopted. When they called him, he behaved oddly. Then, one morning, he finally spoke out: The armistice with Italy had been signed. Of course! Until that moment, Alvise had been an "enemy." He even felt that he was some sort of prisoner of war.

"I would have had to go to a concentration camp. I didn't want to leave you alone."

The very idea of that first-rate ball-breaker ending up in a remote prisoner of war camp filled me with joy. But no, no chance of that.

"I had to see what they were planning to do with you. Now that there's an armistice with Italy, the best thing would be for us to stay together. Yes, I'll ask for you to be sent with me to Ferrara."

I scuffed the floor with my foot. I screwed up my mouth. I swallowed. I scratched my nose. My eye twitched. I scratched my arm. In short, in a single second I was transformed into a carnival of tics.

That charming little plan of his sent chills down my spine. I remembered the Villa Ombreggiata, with its fragrance of candles, those starched governesses. I could hear that violin buzzing in my ears. I could see that painting in which Salome danced with her veils in front of John the Baptist's severed head.

"That way the two of us will always stick together. After all, you've always been like a little brother to me, right, Sammy?"

He had an indescribable expression on his face. His eyes emitted turquoise flashes of sparkling virtue. His blond, clean hair glowed like a halo over his head. I nodded slowly and mechanically, as if guided by the weight of my big nose. Then, I ran to hide myself in a shit-hole of a latrine.

I didn't put it that way out of vulgarity. It just happened to be a foul, stinking hole, probably intended for "third class" immigrants. This hole was a little wooden closet behind a storage room full of partitions. I had to sneak past a small shed that must have been a guardroom, to finally make it to the latrine. I hid there with twenty bars of chocolate and a pile of marvelous Mickey Mouse comic books.

I stayed there for three days. A friendly accomplice of mine named Geneviève, or rather, Jenny—a nice kid with round, Harold Lloyd-type glasses, who had a nose twice the size of mine—finally gave me some peace of mind by telling me that Alvise had left.

"Some gentleman in a fancy suit came to take him away. I think he was a count or something. They looked for you all over the place, and they said they'd be back to look for you again."

It was because of this threat that I decided to undergo, for the first time in my life, my virgin experience as a whore.

I began to look among the prospective parents who stood behind the barriers. I chose a couple who were not only plump—which meant they probably ate well at home—but also kind, which meant I could do what I wanted; and also ugly, which meant that *I* could finally be the pretty one in the house.

I stood in front of them. I began to gaze intensely at the woman, who looked something like a Mack truck in polka-dots. I smiled tenderly and winked at her. It must have moved her deeply, because she immediately elbowed a squat figure beside her who, though short, was wide as a house—a house with a garage. He had a large, gray hat and a familiar *shnoz*. Then the woman smiled at me, and everything was set.

Hold on. To tell it like it was, I should mention a little detail: I exchanged the number on my chart with that of another child, and then I threw my number out of the window into the river. I hadn't planned on leaving any traces behind, because I never wanted Alvise to find me again. Then, I skipped out of that place with my new parents and—after such a long time—well, I finally felt back in my own place; in other words, like a normal little boy. *Me.*

Later, in the lobby of the immigration office, I saw Alvise again. He was there with the distinguished gentleman, in the midst of the crowd, still looking for me and calling my name:

"Sam. Sam . . ."

New York, Forty Years Later

"The successful man *is* a Ferrari."

THE WORDS ON THE BILLBOARD suddenly slide before my eyes.

It is an elegant sixty-by-twenty-foot billboard displaying a photograph of a gold Ferrari driven by a sporty gentleman with a pipe, a scarf and a cashmere sweater.

How true it is! "The successful man *is* a Ferrari." In fact, it is a Ferrari identical to the one in the billboard that is gliding down the streets of midtown Manhattan, driven by none other than old Sammy—I mean, me! I mean a guy who resembles the man on the billboard. I mean, I keep myself in step. I not only have my Ferrari, but I also have my Dunhill pipe—the pipe for the connoisseur; my Balkan Sobranie tobacco—the tobacco for the virile man; my Old England scarf—cashmere for the man with class; my Gucci shoes—for the true gentleman; my Vuitton attaché case, and so on, down to my shorts.

Let's get something straight. I don't believe in advertising, I have a blind, subliminal faith in it. I don't look up to it. I idolize it. I don't oppose it. I let myself be swept away by it. I don't argue. I obey.

Yes! In this consumer society, I am what you call an ideal consumer, an ideal citizen, an ideal man.

I find it proper, patriotic and very comfortable to design my look and my personality according to what SHE—advertising—dictates.

This is a luxury I can allow myself, because I am a "successful man."

The products in advertisements are not cheap, and you wouldn't find them in a bargain basement; you need quite a lot of dough, and you have to pay through the nose for that stuff. But, as I said, I can afford it.

Nobody ever catches me out of fashion. I mean . . .

Nobody ever caught me back then, when I was a happy man . . . before everything snapped.

I was enjoying life in old Manhattan like a rat in a big hunk of cheese. Life was smiling at me that morning when I looked up at the billboard. I didn't realize what a happy man I was back then.

What is happiness, after all? It's not an easy word to define. It's something impalpable . . . a sweet breeze, a certain situation. Let me try to explain it to you: Here I come with my car, right? I drop off my Ferrari with old Tony, the garage attendant. He waves at me and even adds a little bow. He just adores my car, and he's still holding on to my autograph along with the first dollar bill I ever gave him.

I walk on and pause in front of the corner bookstore. There is an entire display of thrillers. On every cover is a picture of a nude woman with black stockings, holding a machine gun. The title is unforgettable: *Mike Bullit Up Against the Blond Hyena.* A classic. On the back of the book is the author's face. Sam Silverman—I mean me, of course. There I am, posing like an intellectual and country gentleman, with my pipe, scarf and golden retriever.

Well, maybe this is what happiness means: starting off the morning with thirty-two images of yourself smiling at you! Let's just say it's a situation of privilege. You feel like you're at the top.

A successful man. A man who's made it. A man who knows how to make good money. A man who pays high taxes. A man who's got one of the best jobs around: fabricating dreams and fantasies for the common people.

Yesssir! Psychiatrists and sociologists swear that if violence is under control in big cities, it's because of men like me. People read my books full of sex and tough stuff, they vent their ferocious, destructive instincts while reading, and then they're able to go to bed feeling calm and relaxed. So, without false modesty, I play an important role in society.

People love me, they adore me. My books are sold by the thousand, like McDonald's hamburgers.

That means a lot of money piling up in my personal bank account. With it, I am able to pay those criminal taxes, and there is even enough left over to allow me to sail through this vale of tears without too much discomfort.

As a matter of fact, I can lament the vanity of life and

await a heart attack with a certain amount of ease. That is, I could back then.

That morning, unaware and happy, I am just walking along the road. Hey, guys—watch out! I'm using the present narrative tense, not out of ignorance, but in order to pay tribute to Damon Runyon—the great master.

Stuck on the implacable television screens of twenty TV sets in an appliance and hi-fi store window are twenty identical replicas of the talk show host who is confidentially greeting me, along with millions of other Americans.

"Good morning, America!"

"Good morning, TV," I respond with a wink. I'm feeling self-assured and contented.

I too am America.

Actually, I particularly am America. I'm one of the most solid pillars of this great, neurotic, democratic society.

You find my self-assurance irritating, don't you? That's normal, but you must understand that I've got something special. Yeah . . .

I stop to check myself out in the reflection of a store window. Well, maybe I'm not what you'd call gorgeous, but whattya want? I mean, for an intellectual, a successful writer, it isn't bad. An interesting face . . . elegant, slim, sporty. Intelligent, expressive eyes. A sarcastic little smile on the edge of my lips. And then, yeah, I have to admit it—dames really go for me. Let's face it. I'm sorry, I know it may come as a shock to you—but the broads really like me, and you know in what way! I'm considered sexy. I've been famous since college days. They used to call me "the beast." Hey, do you catch my drift?

Many girls came out of curiosity, and no one left disappointed. I lured the dolls away from six-foot-tall blond tennis champs who resembled Robert Redford. It was known. Everybody talked about it.

"How does he do it?" people would ask. Girls would gossip and tell stories about me while washing their hair or painting their toenails.

What it comes down to is that I'm super-endowed. It happens sometimes to Jews with delicate, discreet appearances. And in that sense, too, I guess you could say I'm a successful man.

Two girls are looking at me. They probably recognize me. I wink at them, and the dolls giggle.

It's just in that moment of pure bliss that I suddenly feel I'm being watched. I glance around. I catch sight of a man across the sidewalk who's staring at me.

That's how it all begins. From that gaze. In the beginning, I hardly notice it. I turn away from the man's fixed stare.

Then, I turn around again, and look at him with a delayed reaction, in the style of Edward Everett Horton. After a moment, the man drops his eyes in embarrassment and takes a few steps. Then he pauses and looks at me once again. I have to avert my eyes this time. Well, you know how it is when two people are looking at each other.

The man is strange. There is something interesting about him. Tall, with a grizzled beard, he looks intelligent. He might remind you of Hemingway. Perhaps he had a more free and easy quality about him. He had charisma. He had some kind of aura. Something Lawrence of Arabia must have had, or Orson Welles, or Fellini, or even certain painters such as Picasso and Michelangelo.

He's wearing a Russian shirt with a leather belt hung low, which gives prominence to his lean and handsome figure. An old threadbare jacket—elegant without exaggeration—brings everything back to normality. His style is quite eccentric but not too flamboyant, and certainly not fashionable. There is neither Gucci, nor Old England. He is elegant in an unusual way. Even his beard and windswept hair give him a romantic look.

I suddenly feel a little twinge in my guts. I don't realize what it is right away. Then I suspect it must be a pang of envy.

I continue walking, trying not to think about it. Nothing happens. It's only someone watching me. He's a little out of the ordinary. An interesting man. Period. I can't resist the temptation, and I take another look.

The man looks at me once again, and then we both avert our eyes at the same time. I'm beginning to feel a little apprehensive. I quicken my pace. Yes, after all, as I said before, I've always been successful with women— especially those who are experienced with the erotic, with epicurean tastes and a touch of sophistication. As for men, forget it! I'm not their type. I've never had anything to do with Midnight Cowboys, pansy queens or faggot Casanovas. No doubt about that!

I just can't figure out why that guy keeps staring at me. Then, after a while, I begin to realize that he's actually following me.

He's several feet behind me, walking along with the morning crowd on Fifth Avenue.

I pause and pretend to look at a display window. The man stops in front of another window. I venture a stealthy look, and once again our eyes meet for a moment.

I start walking again. The man does the same.

I begin to get nervous.

I go into a bar belonging to an old pal of mine named Billy.

The strange man walks past the bar.

It has to be my imagination! He wasn't following me.

"It was pure imagination! Thank God!"

Billy teases me.

"Hey, Sam, ya talkin' to yourself?"

"No, it's just that . . ."

I signal to Billy to come closer and speak in a low voice. I lean over the counter toward him. Billy leans over too. I whisper excitedly into his ear as I cleverly pick his pocket.

"Somebody's following me. Must be the CIA."

"Oh, yeah?!"

I look around and wink at him, and then continue in a normal voice.

"Listen, I don't have any change on me. You couldn't lend me five bucks, could you?"

"Sure, right away, buddy."

He feels his pocket but doesn't find his wallet. He begins to search his other pockets frantically.

"Oh, Christ. Oh, Christ. Oh Christ, oh Christ."

"Hey, whattya tryin' to do, convert me or something? Look, forget it. Looks like I'll have to lend *you* five bucks, okay?"

I'm completely nonchalant as I take out his wallet and open it under his nose. Billy is sweating and his eyes are popping out. Then he realizes, points to the wallet and stammers.

"Hey! But that, that's mine."

"'Course it is!" I laugh, and tap the wallet on his head as I give it back to him.

"You're a real *schmuck*, Billy. Learn to be on your toes a little more, eh?"

Billy doesn't know whether to laugh or protest.

"Ah, Christ. Enough to give a guy a heart attack. What a shitty trick."

" 'Bye, 'bye, baby . . . 'I can't give you anything but love . . .' "

I leave the bar singing and laughing.

Oh, NO!

Oh, yes, the mystery man is waiting outside for me, in front of a shop window.

I gasp but walk away as if nothing has happened. The man follows me.

There's no longer any doubt about it. He's got something on me. As an author of thrillers, I'm used to the idea of shadowing. It's my daily bread. But it's one thing to write it, and another to experience it. I feel more nervous than ever. And when I feel nervous, all my childhood tics begin to surface. I scratch myself. My shoulders jerk. My eyebrows twitch. I screw up my mouth. Fortunately, being a theoretical expert in shadowing, I soon manage to shake him off my trail.

A professional job, chums—it's practically child's play.

I stop in front of a shop window. He stops too. I walk back. He follows. I enter a familiar shop I know has two exits, and leave from the other door. I run down the steps of a subway station in the midst of a sea of people. Then I reemerge from another exit. The game is all over. I've shaken him off.

What did you think, mysterious man? Did you think you'd fool old Sammy?

My publishing house stands out, imperceptibly swaying along its ninety-story spine in the morning ocean breeze. I smell that fresh air that has combed through trees in the park and is now swirling around that gigantic, beaconlike building of plate glass.

I cross the crowded lobby and head for the elevators.

I suddenly sense there is someone behind me. Who could it be? Yes, it was him again: my pursuer. The mysterious, bearded man catches up with me. He enters the same lobby of the same building, at the same time. Then he follows me to the elevators.

I must admit I feel bewildered. I stand still. But the crowds push me into the elevator. The elevator fills up immediately, the doors close, the buttons are pushed, and the voyage begins.

I find myself face-to-face and eyeball-to-eyeball with the bearded guy. Destiny's design is complete. A spark. A puff of smoke. A mystical vision. A visitation. A flashback.

A memory shoots through my mind which I draw up from the black well of my childhood subconscious.

The cold steel of the elevator walls is suddenly transformed into warm wood and ground-crystal arabesques. There are images of nymphs and fauns among clusters of grapes.

There are the window panes of the Villa Ombreggiata. Rays of sunlight filter through the panes onto the painting of "The Dance of Salome." The prophet's severed head lies on a silver platter. A beautiful fair-haired child is playing the violin divinely.

He draws out the last passionate note with his bow and opens his enraptured eyes. He follows my gaze to the painting.

"Do you like John, the prophet? Salome dances in front of King Herod because she wants the head of John the Baptist."

Forty years have passed . . .

It seems like a century.

A century, in a flash. The memories of an entire life have sped through my mind as I gaze at the intense, bearded face, the face of Alvise.

"Sammy."

The elevator stops on the thirtieth floor.

"It's me. Alvise."

Alvise . . .

Salome's violent and sinuous dance echoes in my head. The sounds of the languid, imperious violins become frenzied.

The elevator doors open. We are pushed out with the crowd.

We are nailed to the floor, face-to-face, eyeball-to-eyeball.

"Sammy."

"Alvise!"

We hug each other.

"Sammy."

"Alvise."

Just then, a woman, built like a battleship, with an embarrassingly ample tush, waddles down the hall. Still hugging Alvise, I watch her slacken her pace as she passes us.

She studies us severely through a gold lorgnette, and a look of disgust comes over her face.

She keeps her eyes on us as she walks off. Surely, she'll tell someone: how shameful, two grown men kissing each other.

An open-minded errand boy winks at us, however. I'm beginning to feel a bit embarrassed.

We draw apart. Alvise looks at me tenderly.

"Sammy. It's been so long . . ."

He can't take his eyes off me.

So there we are, in the corridor of the publishing house on the thirtieth floor, standing in front of the enormous glass display case. My books are there, just below the center of the case, below the place of honor reserved for the Nobel Prize-winning book.

Alvise pats me affectionately on the back.

His intelligent eyes sparkle with warmth.

"How are you? What are you doing?"

I point out my books to him. My photograph can be seen on the back cover. My false modesty is even less convincing than usual.

"Oh, living, working."

Alvise's face breaks into a smile of amazement and delight.

"Oh, I know! Of course! Congratulations, Sam, congratulations. It's extraordinary. You've become a star."

Well, I must confess that makes me happy. But I hide my vanity by playing the whole thing down.

"A star? Let's not exaggerate! I just write escape fiction, thrillers. Yeah, I get thousands of letters from my fans and all that crap. But it's only light reading, the minor leagues."

"No, no. It's not minor at all. Bravo! You've done very well. I'm really proud of you! Congratulations!"

He pauses for a moment and smiles with a trace of embarrassment.

"I had a book published too."

"Oh?"

I blink in bewilderment. I try to remember something he might have done, but nothing comes to mind. Nevertheless, I wasn't about to lose any points.

"Ah . . . yes? Sorry, I didn't . . ."

Alvise interrupts with a charming smile.

"You couldn't have seen my name. I used a pseudonym. But we're part of the same team."

The publisher and his staff are padding silently over the thick, plush carpet.

The publisher's face breaks into a smile as soon as he recognizes Alvise.

"Professor . . . You know Sammy? This old rascal? How on earth?"

I can't deny it. I feel deflated by the publisher's arrival. I instinctively assume subordinate dimensions, while I notice with amazement that Alvise, with his splendid simplicity, has grown in stature.

It's obvious at first sight that the publisher is a doormat at Alvise's feet. He simply fawns over him, and then, to kiss his ass better, he draws me in too.

"What can there ever be in common between our Mike Bullit and you? Don't tell me that even Sammy reads Isaac Smith!"

"Oh, we're old childhood friends. Bound together for life and death."

"Is that so? Well, well. Ah! By the way, what do you think of the publicity? The Nobel Prize doesn't happen every day."

Don't ask me about the rest of the conversation. I switched off my earphones. My mouth drops open in shock. Struck by lightning.

Alvise looks at me and probably goes on talking. But I only hear my croaking, echoing voice asking the incredible question.

"Isaac Smith? You're Isaac Smith? The Nobel Prize winner?!"

Alvise has the same blithe, modest smile that has always made Gary Cooper irresistible. Remember?

"Isaac Smith. I thought it sounded like a good name. A common Jewish first name combined with the most ordinary Anglo-Saxon surname."

Everything snaps!!!!

He points to the long procession of finely bound volumes.

Man Could Be Beautiful, by Isaac Smith.

"Winner of the Nobel Prize. A masterpiece of contemporary poetry" says the book jacket.

A Malayan Kriss dagger, with its ridged, serpentine blade, twists in my guts as I read those words.

The publisher goes on talking, and Alvise goes on smiling. I try to hide the fact that I'm turning green, with poisonous bile rising inside me. I can hear the blood roaring in my ears.

The Nobel Prize! Alvise was Isaac Smith, the Nobel Prize winner of the year.

I'm locked inside my study. State of emergency. I'm in the throes of a total crisis. My wife, Alice, is screaming at me from the other side of the door.

Screaming is my wife's way of dealing with her hysteria and paranoia. She knows very well that she won't get anything out of me by screaming. But she's already tried everything else—kindness, rudeness, sweetness and threats. Nothing worked. Screaming was the only choice she had left.

It's useless, I don't want to write anymore. I was used to writing one mystery book a month. Not only was I used to it, but so was my publishing house, Alice the wifey, and the entire organization. Now it's over.

Now they have to leave me alone.

I don't want to write anymore.

Mysteries and thrillers belong to an industrial, commercial branch of publishing—mass-market books. And I? How did I get into it? Yeah, sure! With the sadness of one who had other ambitions. Nevertheless, it brought me certain comforts, pleasant habits, fans, credit, high taxes and a consoling bank account.

Comfort conditions a man, and when you have to write a thriller a month, you don't have time for any artistic identity crises.

In other words, I hadn't been badly off at all. I mean, yeah, I felt like I'd made it big. People would say: "Hey, there goes Mike Bullit!"

People were proud to know me. They patted my back. They envied me, and all the rest.

Lawyers, executives, doctors . . . I'd seen their eyes sparkle with admiration. Behind me stood Edgar Wallace, Ian Fleming, Agatha Christie and Simenon. Those people were really on the ball, and they protected me. It takes a special person to write thrillers, all right. Not everyone can do it. And to think I had hit it so big!

But it's all over. Everything has collapsed.

My study is bolted shut.

Alice is distressed, and stubbornly continues to knock at my door.

"Sammy! Sammy . . . Be good . . . Open up."

But my door stays shut.

With a worried face and eyes brimming with tears, Alice turns to Doctor Floodrestein and shakes her head.

Shapiro, a guy from the publishing house, stands next to her.

"No way. It's been two days now, he won't open up.

He won't eat. Nothing. What do you think is wrong with him, Doctor?"

"Nothing. I wouldn't worry about it, I'm sure it's just stress. Fatigue. A successful writer who drives himself to keep up with success. It's probably just a case of exhaustion."

"But he doesn't want to write anymore. He was supposed to hand over his monthly mystery yesterday."

Shapiro smiles, his jowls trembling like an old mastiff's.

"Don't worry Alice. Mr. Morgan was very understanding. He said Sammy could skip this month."

Alice is pale and tense as she presses her ear against the door.

"Do you hear?"

"I can't hear anything."

"Exactly. He sits perfectly still and never budges."

Yeah, sure! I've been barricaded at my desk, in my study, for two whole days.

I sit there, petrified. My eyes are sunken, and I have dark circles under them. My lips are sealed tight, and my skin has a greenish tinge to it. A series of tics rouse me from my torpor every now and then: My nose twitches, my head shakes, my shoulders jerk, I itch. These convulsive moments are all that interrupt my feverish immobility. I look like an anomalous Buddha.

I hear Alice's voice whining behind the door.

"Sammy! Sammy, open up. There's someone here who's got to talk to you. Sammy . . . Sammy . . . Sammy . . . Sammy . . . Sammy . . ."

How can anyone go on repeating someone's name

like a broken record? The sound of it drives me crazy.

I can't take it any longer. I spring up with my eyes bulging out of my head, and begin to yell.

"Stop iiiit! For Chrissakes! Doesn't a man have the right to be left in peace for just a little while?!"

But that crazy Alice just goes on yelling louder than me.

"You've been in there for two days like a lunatic! Doctor Floodrestein is here. A wife has the right—"

With a violent leap, I reach for the door and push it open. Alice, Doctor Floodrestein and Shapiro are all standing there like three cretins. Alice, who is still yelling, lowers her voice.

"Don't get mad, Sammy. We only want to help you. Here is—"

"I know who's here. Let's not pretend that I can't make an educated guess. You've hardly called in an electrician!"

Then I turn to the doctor.

"I just want to warn you. I never gave a cent to an analyst. That's what you are, aren't you?"

Doctor Floodrestein nods at me with one of those stereotyped fatherly grins. I won't let him get a word in edgewise.

"Great. Know why? I mean, why I don't shell out to analysts? I'll tell you. I don't get lapses. I don't have sexual problems. I stopped masturbating at thirteen. My relationships with my parents—the real ones and the adoptive ones—were terrific. No Oedipus complexes—I was never in love with either of my mothers, nor did I dream of having a fling with my grandmother. I never saw my parents making love. I never thought of having any incestuous and homosexual relationships with my uncles. No, nobody's ever caught me on that little couch. I'm the only citizen in this state with an income over two hundred thousand dollars a year who's never been forced down on any of those bloodsuckers' couches."

Doctor Floodrestein interrupts me by raising his hand.

"I understand. I'll be leaving. Madam."

He straightens his hat and heads for the door. I can't hold it back.

"Give my regards to Freud."

Alice glares at me.

"Sammy! Excuse him, Doctor Floodrestein. At least send me the bill for your trouble."

The doctor turns around and gives Alice a typical jackal smile.

"Certainly, Madam. I may be persona non grata here, but I'm not gratis. I'll be going now. Good-bye."

He closes the door politely behind him. I turn to Shapiro with a sneer. Shapiro knows me, and jumps in.

"All right, all right, Sammy. I'm going. I don't want anything. Don't worry. We'll skip this month, okay? You can give us the next mystery the following month, okay?"

"No, *bubeleh*. Not the next month, or ever again. And you can go and tell that to those vultures at the office. I'm through. Bullit is dead. I'm finished writing. I'm through!"

I go back into the study and slam the door in his face.

I don't notice that my wife is in the study with me. In silence, I go and sit down at my desk again.

Gloomily, I stare at Alvise's book, which lies on the desk in front of me. Alice watches me worriedly. I become aware of her presence. I fume.

"Do I have to shoot myself to get a little peace around here?!"

"You haven't eaten anything in days, darling."

"I'm not hungry."

"I have some homemade chicken soup."

"I'd rather have an enema."

"Shall I whip up an egg with some sugar and a little mint syrup? You've always liked mint zabaione so much."

She goes over to the brass-studded, leather-lined bar. She takes an egg, gets out the sugar and mint, and starts to make the zabaione. I feel queasy—the glop is a sickening shade of green.

Alice shakes her head in her maternal, patient way as she beats the egg yolk with the sugar and mint.

"What is it? I'm your wife, Sammy. I love you. Why don't you get it off your chest?"

She comes over to me and touches my shoulder. I shudder.

Alice draws back, frightened. She goes back to beating the zabaione with a look of anguish on her face.

Someone knocks at the door.

"Don't open it."

I can hear the teasing, silvery voice of my son, Chucky, on the other side of the door.

"Hey, Calagan! Ya want me to sneak ya some food?"

Calagan is a famous inspector who appears in many of my novels. Chipper, my little daughter, screams too.

"The old witch ain't around."

"The old witch *is* around!" Alice snarls as she opens the door. Her face has turned green. She knows that our children have always been my accomplices, and that they call her "the old witch" to amuse me.

I'm always indulgent toward the mischievous, rebellious side of my children. In any case, there's always Alice around to bitch and to badger them with discipline and teach them proper manners. This friendly conspiracy of ours drives her nuts, which is why "the old witch" nervously shoos them away.

"Come on, go do your homework, kids. Daddy's not feeling well."

Chucky manages to wink at me before the door closes behind him.

My kids are really on the ball. I feel a little ashamed of myself, and of all that is happening to me. Poor little things, they're so funny and cute.

When they find out that tough Mike Bullit, Old Calagan—their hero and their pride among their friends at school—is nothing but a measly scribbler of cheap thrillers . . . Yeah, you can bet on it, they'll be ashamed of me when they grow up.

And when somebody asks them, "What did your father do?"—they'll start stuttering and inventing stories. "Oh, he was a farmer in Kentucky, strong as an ox." Or perhaps: "Oh, poor old Dad, he gambled away Grandpa's entire fortune. He ended up as a magician in country fairs."

Then, they'll get to know other fathers. They might meet someone like Alvise, and then my own mediocrity will turn them into neurotics with massive inferiority complexes. They'll probably seek security in drugs. They'll start with the light stuff first, and then get into the heavy stuff. The police will call on me one night.

I'll find my son on a sidewalk in the slums, lying in the trash like a worthless rag. He'll be dying from an overdose, and I'll ask him:

"Why, Chucky? Why?"

He won't answer me, but I'll see the terrible condemnation in my son's eyes.

Like an old fool, I'll run and throw myself into the Hudson River.

Alice's voice suddenly interrupts my gloomy fantasies.

"It's because of that old friend of yours you saw again, isn't it?"

I jump at the sound of her voice. She points to the book and goes on beating the zabaione.

Once again I shudder. My teeth are chattering. I try to get a hold of myself, but the tics go off in succession.

"Who? Alvise? No, of course not. What's he got to do with this?"

Alice is watching me. She knows me.

She also notices my clumsy attempt to hide the book.

"Is that the book that won the Nobel Prize? Have you read it?"

The tics get more and more frantic, but I continue to feign indifference.

"Hmmm? No, I haven't had the time. I just gave it a quick glance."

"Is it any good?

"Mmm. Maybe. A little boring."

"Why don't you tell me the truth, Sammy? You're full of tics."

I look at her with hatred.

"Don't bug me, dammitall! Please. I've got a lot on my mind! I've got a creative block. I'm up shit creek without a paddle. And I wanna be left alone!"

Alice stands in front of me and looks me straight in the eye.

"You're writhing like a worm. Tell me the truth, Sammy. You did read it didn't you? Is it any good?"

I shudder miserably. I wince and double over in pain.

"Shut up! Stop it!"

An icy grip gets hold of my stomach and begins to twist it.

"Is it any good?"

I throw off my disguise.

"No! It's not good at all! It's magnificent! It's the most magnificent thing I've read in twenty years. Oh, God! Oh, God!"

"And yet it makes you double over in pain?"

"Shut up! I just can't stand the idea that he's a great poet!"

"But, Sammy, that's horrible. It can't be. Someone might say that you're jealous. Are you jealous?"

And there she is, in front of me, beating the damn zabaione with that stupid sincerity of hers.

"Of course! Does that seem normal to you? The Nobel Prize?!"

"So? Then you should admire him, since you say it's

so magnificent. You almost sound like you hate him. Do you hate him?" She goes on beating that egg glop.

"Of course I hate him. I feel like a worm! A piece of shit! A failure! That bastard has made me feel like hell!"

"Come on. Try to get a hold of yourself, darling. Force yourself to get back to work. You'll see, you'll get over it. Try."

She continues to beat that goddam green *dreck*. Who was it that said that green is the color of envy?

"You're a nitwit. What's with you? Can't you see there's an earthquake bursting inside of me? My life is crumbling. And you think that a guy who's lying crushed under the rubble of his destroyed being can sit down quietly and write stuff like: 'Don Flaherty advanced through the darkness, while the barrels of the revolvers pointed at him like eyes in the night'?"

"Don't be unfair, Sam. You've done wonderful work. You're admired. Everybody knows you and admires you —maybe even too well—friends, men, women. They invite you everywhere. You're a big success!"

Alice finally hands me the mint zabaione. I take it and send the whole cup crashing to the floor.

"I'm a successful piece of shit. That stuff is nothing but shit. I'm a *schmuck!* Just a hack writer of *schlock!* A real *schmuck!* I screwed up everything. Because I used to write well . . . I had things to say. I had great possibilities."

But Alice isn't listening. She only gazes at her carpet, which is now soiled with that greenish-yellow *dreck*.

"You've dirtied the carpet."

"Yeah. That carpet, that *"noisette-*brown" carpet. Yeah, sure! That expensive French stuff—paid for with the earnings of *I'll Kiss You, I'll Shoot You*—sixty-seven thousand copies sold. Do you know that it's all your fault?!"

"My fault? What's my fault?!"

"Yes! Yours! With your carpet! And this apartment! All sixteen hundred square feet of it, that swallowed up the rights of *Don't Try It, Mike*—three hundred thousand copies sold. Then came the furniture, Gucci, the mink, the cruises, the oak paneling, Georgette Klinger, the masseuse, the country club, the Philippine maid, the parties, the color TV, the rollerskates, the Ferrari. And all that other crap advertising urges you to buy. Yeah, that's why I wrote a book a month. I'm just a scumbag, and you . . . you . . ."

"Me? Calm down, sweetie. Let's get it straight, angel face. You liked all this stuff too, and so much so, that when we got married, you hardly warned me that you wanted to live in a hovel and make like a poet!"

"Women are supposed to have intuition about certain things."

"About what things, you idiot? I had to have some intuition about the fact that money didn't interest you? Hah! You were crazy about it! You got turned on every time you touched a dollar bill. And what a tightwad you were! Weren't you the one who invented the 'urgent' phone calls in the restaurant when the check came around? And who made collect calls to my father's house when we were engaged?"

"Great! Now it all comes out! I've nursed a viper in my bosom!"

"You've always been interested in money, sweetie!

You even counted on a generous cash wedding present from my parents! No! At least don't start playing the hypocrite. You always loved money and all the rest. And let's get this straight—you were already writing this stuff when I met you, remember? 'Hey, doll, you've got a pair of thirty-eight caliber tits! Don't shoot 'em in my face!' "

"It was my first novel, published for a competition by the *Sunday Mountain Chronicle*. I won a thousand bucks which paid for my vacation in Santa Barbara, where you were waiting for me on that beach, ready to sink your hooks into me."

"Me? I was going to college there. I had a career."

"Yeah, as a dentist. What a vocation."

"It's an honorable profession. It's important and scientific, even if you always did have to put it down. Yes! I had to fall in love with you like an idiot, and you destroyed my career. Do you realize that now I'm here as your slave, working as your secretary, keeping your bills together? Cleaning your carpet?"

Sure enough, the bitch goes down on her hands and knees and begins cleaning the carpet. And you can bet she feels like a slave. But I'm not gonna fall for it!

"No, my love. You don't limit yourself to cleaning carpets, you buy them. You don't limit yourself to managing the money, you spend it by the truckload. And what's more, with that loser of an accountant we've got, you don't even let me deduct those expenses from taxes."

Alice goes off on a tangent at this point.

"For godsake!! Don't start all over with that seventy

thousand dollars! It cannot be considered part of your business expenses, and therefore it is not tax deductible."

I go right after her, because the subject drives me crazy.

"Why not? If we spent it, why can't we put it down as part of our expenses? Christ!"

"My God, sometimes it seems like you're retarded, Sammy!"

Alice, that bitch of a moron, starts with her terrible "common sense" tone.

Now, just tell me if there's anything worse than common sense. That's what makes you want to set your schoolteachers on fire, or put sticks of dynamite under your aunt's house. Common sense is what nourishes anarchists and international terrorism. Common sense drives everyone nuts. As for Alice, when she starts putting on her teacher's common-sense act, she busts your balls no end.

"It seems like you're retarded!"

She wants to convince me that, not only is she right, but also the accountant, the bloodsucking government and the whole system are right. Instead, it is obvious that they are all wrong.

"Excuse me, why does it seem like I'm retarded?"

She explains it to me with the shrill tone of a pedantic shrew.

"You seem retarded because you pretend not to understand. The vacation in Yucatán . . . the Modigliani drawing . . . the Gucci bill . . . and the Krizia dress are not tax de-duc-ti-ble! Do you get that?! They cannot be listed as tax-deductible expenses for business purposes."

"What do you mean they're not for business purposes!? What the hell! I'm not representing a company after all; I'm representing Sammy Silverman. I can hardly have everyone saying Silverman's wife is wearing some chintzy costume from Macy's bargain basement! Or that my walls are covered with stenciled flowers. This whole dump is a business expense! Your mink is a business expense!"

"Oh, no, you couldn't possibly leave out my mink! Some day I'm going to burn that coat!"

Her words don't register anymore.

"They're all business expenses I need for my image."

I suddenly realize the great truth of those words.

"It's true. That's the way I project myself. I, a man, have a certain image. These expenses are necessary to maintain that image. It's horrible! Horrible! But at least they should be tax deductible."

"No. With four hundred and forty-six thousand copies sold, face it, Sammy, you've got to pay taxes."

To hell with her and her taxes.

This business about taxes makes me wild with rage. My crisis reaches the breaking point and, pissed as hell, I begin to roar.

"I'm a loser! I've failed as a man! Can't you see that? Taxes. Expenses. Vulgarity. I was an artist! I was born to fly, to scale the heights and smile. To be a connoisseur of ecstasies, to write poetry . . ."

I look at Alvise's book. I grab it and examine its jacket. *A million copies sold.*

A thought flashes through my mind.

"Yeah. A million copies sold. God bless poetry, see

what it can do? A million copies. And how much does *he* pay in taxes?"

My eyes stare into Alice's, but I don't see her.

The idea begins to grab a hold of me. I seize the telephone. I dial a number. Alice doesn't take her eyes off me.

"What's popped into your head now?"

"I'm calling our famous tax specialist. Isn't our Billy an expert in the investigations field? I'd like to find out how our perfect Alvise deals with his taxes. His family was already loaded before the war, and now that he's got all those royalties, you can just imagine. I bet he's got an account in Switzerland.

"Yes? Is this the Internal Revenue Service? Billy, is that you? Listen, I gotta know how much a certain person pays in taxes. Yes . . . an Italian. I know. I know they make a big mess out of taxes down there, but I don't care about the cost. I've got to know. The guy's name is Isaac Smith. Yes, he's Jewish. You heard of him? Sure. He's the one who won the Nobel Prize for poetry this year. Yeah, the Nobel Prize."

While I am busy trying to get that thickheaded Billy to understand what I want, the other telephone rings. Alice answers it.

"Oh, Jesus Christ, don't you know what the Nobel Prize is? No, Billy! It's not some sort of Oscar. All right, never mind. Isaac Smith is a pseudonym. Write down his real name. He's an aristocrat, a count. Alvise Ottolenghi Portaleoni. Yes, Billy, there are also Jewish aristocrats in Europe!"

Guess who's calling on the other phone?

Yes! Speak of the devil. It's Alvise.

Alice's face lights up in excitement as she speaks in her most "cultivated" voice.

"Yes? Ah. I'm Alice, Sammy's wife. Of course. I think so. Sammy? Alvise wants to know if we can all have dinner together tonight. You and I with him and his wife."

Well, of course! How could I expect Alvise's wife to be anything less than splendid? I knew it. I expected it.

When the restaurant doors open, and Alvise and his wife come in, I am prepared.

Alice and I, all spruced up and on our best behavior, are waiting for them at a table. We obviously have to look our best. Alice is wearing a designer dress and has had her hair done. I'm wearing my most elegant, conservative tie.

Alice takes the event as a sign of my convalescence, poor fool, but the truth is that I only came out dressed to kill in order to stock up on ammunition.

I am pissed as hell. In addition to the throes of my identity crisis and existential rage, I now discover yet another source of irritation—Alice is extremely excited, panting like a dog in heat about meeting a Nobel Prize winner. I had to scream and make her cry before we were even able to enter the restaurant.

As always, seeing her unhappy brings me some peace of mind. I feel better and ready for battle.

The smile freezes on my face when I catch sight of Alvise's wife. She is young, blond, and golden-eyed. As she comes closer, she emits a glow, an aura. It may be her dress, her fair hair, her perfume or her chiffon veils. She floats through the people and the waiters, barely touching the ground. It is overwhelming.

I glance at my Alice and compare her to the blond phoenix who now holds out her hand to me. In reality, her pale hand is a dying swan on a lake, by a grove of weeping willows with choreography by George Balanchine!

Of course! How can Alvise's wife be anything but perfect? How can her name be anything but Dorothea?!

She's a phoenix, a swan, an angel, divine and simple. She caresses me with an amused gaze from her golden eyes.

Alice isn't even aware of her presence. And why not? Elementary, my dear Watson: She has been struck by lightning. She has been in a state of ecstasy from the first moment she laid eyes on Alvise. I expected that. It isn't surprising that she's all bright eyes and bushy tail in front of him, the little idiot.

"You know, it's so exciting! You're the first Nobel Prize winner I ever met!"

"Oh, please!"

Fortunately, Dorothea prefers the earthly to the Olympian.

"Oh, this business with the Nobel Prize! It's become such an obsession! I'm sick of it. Actually, my favorite books are thrillers. I adore them. They're relaxing and fun to read. *Littérature engagée* has become such a bore. I'm an admirer of yours, Sammy. Now, I want to know everything. How do you go about inventing all those riveting stories?"

"Oh, it's mere child's play."

I must admit, I am very flattered. I speak with animation. I feel elated, I am a brilliant raconteur, and I get back all my spellbinding charm and man-about-town sparkle. The superb blonde's admiration excites me and fills me with satanic ambition.

Certainly. Why not? He has the Nobel Prize. He has rank and title. He has poetry. He has looks. He has the villa in Venice. So, why shouldn't I have his wife?

Suddenly, I hold a special session in the private court of my mind. My prosecuting conscience immediately makes charges against me.

Sure, I tell myself. What's the dream of your envious little heart? To run off with Alvise's wife. You'd like everyone to whisper, "The Nobel Prize winner's wife has gone off with that mystery writer." Yeah, you hope they'll say, "He's a fascinating man, not what you'd call handsome, but he's very, very, very, very attractive." Quit fooling yourself, old pal. They'd probably say, "She must have lost her mind to run off with that mystery hack!" Yes, they'd call you a hack, and they'd say that you were a loser, an absolute nobody. After all, your wife would tell everyone how you felt about Alvise, and they'd all see you for what you really are!

That's right. Why do you want to seduce her? For love? Because of overwhelming passion—the kind that sets your blood on fire, tears at your insides and lights wild flames in your eyes—a selfish, all-consuming passion that sweeps away everything? Or perhaps you've fallen under a spell—a spell that drives you mad, gives you wings, makes you sing at night and wreaks havoc with your life. The kind of ardent infatuation depicted by the Mann brothers: Heinrich, whose bourgeois Professor Unrat is reduced to crowing like a rooster by his "blue angel," and Thomas, whose fastidious von Aschenbach falls victim to Tadzio's blond ringlets, and dies, rouged and mascaraed, on the Lido in Venice. Is it because you're thus infatuated that you want to seduce her? No sir! The pathetic absolute nobody, the hack, the loser, is not in this for anything connected with love or passion. He's only in it because he feels inferior. Get that? In-fe-ri-or!

Alvise's superhuman stature makes you feel inferior. But the fact is: You *are* inferior!

To silence this ball-breaking conscience of mine, I smile at the blond Dorothea and pick up the wine list. I try to sound like Maurice Chevalier in *The Merry Widow*.

"Champagne? Certainly, champagne is not what it used to be. Not at all! Those were other times. The vintage is always better after a war. But you need a world war to do it. Those wonderful, all-out wars like we used to have! A sea of blood made the grape harvests more precious in 1915. The Battle of Marne in 1914, don't you know? After 1943, there were great vintages in forty-four and forty-five. But in these humdrum years of the European Common Market, you have to be content with a modest 1968. Dom Perignon? Taitinger? Or would you prefer a good Franciacorta sixty-nine?"

"Oh, I'm afraid I don't care much for champagne. I prefer wine."

"One doesn't dispute your wishes, milady, one fulfills them. Blanc de Blanc seventy-two?"

We both laugh. It's just like being in one of those silly Restoration comedies, which were sophisticated, bawdy and trivial. Comedies which always dealt with—heh, heh, heh!—cuckolds.

Night advances over the Manhattan skyline on black velvet feet, like a wanton cat. She is my friend, and she works for me.

We go to good old Studio 54 where the colorful crowd dances frenetically to the good old blaring music.

Dorothea and I are having a whiskey at the bar. I make her laugh and she tosses her blond hair against my face. I bend over her neck and gallantly whisper irresistible sweet nothings into her rosy, perfumed ear.

Shit! If only I could understand her! To know what, how . . . Will she go for the rough, hairy type, or for the poet? No, forget the poet, for godsake! That's Alvise's role. That means I also have to forget the intellectual. What about the life of the party? The life of the party would be amusing, but unlikely to arouse a great passion. But then again, rich people get bored and end up preferring those who entertain them.

What about the man of action? Sure, perhaps a mystery writer who lives amid revolvers, gangsters and dead bodies that are found at the bottom of the Hudson River with their feet in cement blocks.

Yeah! That might work! She's crazy about thrillers. She admires me. She hates literary figures. She loves action. She even finds Alvise a bit boring. Of course! It has to be this way! Her amused looks seem to express just that.

I please her. I interest her. I amuse her.

I begin to see a light at the end of the tunnel.

Shivers run down my spine. Fantasies flash through my mind.

A brief, violent, primitive, even brutal, but liberating affair. And afterward, to find a little cabin somewhere, where I'd start a new life. Or else a long, tender romance —slow, sweet, ailing and languishing, to be consumed on a magic mountain, possibly in a sanatorium. I get sick. She comes to me. At night, we are feverish and extremely sensual . . . Everyone knows that tuberculosis brings out a terrible, morbid eroticism. Yes. With Death panting in the bed beside us, we are consumed, damned and destroyed, sweating and together wildly carnal and spiritual.

I blink my eyes to drive away these fantasies, and come back to reality. I must make an effort. If I let myself wander into daydreams, I'll be in one hell of a mess.

Dorothea has gone to fill her glass. I watch her like a jaguar in ambush. As the phoenix heads back, I give her the once-over and wink at her in approval.

"Hey, blondie! Your gears mesh very smoothly."

"What?"

"I was just saying that your gears mesh very smoothly. You have the ideal physique for one of my heroines. Dorothea. Blond, chic, divine, drinks only Blanc de Blanc, and murders her victims with a simple scratch of her long, red, pantherlike nails.

Dorothea laughs. I step on the gas and follow up on my attack.

"Each time she appears, she's a knockout. Her charm overwhelms everyone—gangsters, spies, policemen . . . even the author."

My drooping eyelids are a seducer's classic, like von Stroheim in *Foolish Wife*, softened by a Melvyn Douglas smile. Yes, Melvyn Douglas, Garbo's sophisticated partner. The divine blonde is very amused.

Alvise is back at the table talking to Alice, serious and involved.

Dorothea's eyes cast out transparent blue-green flashes. Ah! Of course, Magritte! Her eyes are like cutouts. Two holes through which you can look to the other side, like the eyes in Magritte's paintings. But in the eyes of the painter's figures, you see skies, clouds, birds, while in Dorothea's there is an emerald sea, with violet depths —and possibly sea monsters. Her heavy lashes veil those clear waters with a shady, deceptive mystery. Scary sea caverns. There might be something obscure and morbid about her. I am intrigued. I provoke her, and she laughs.

"Gallant and charming. Thank God. See, that's why I like your stories. They're funny. And then, in a world that's so horribly violent, the violence in the thrillers is relaxing and escapist, like fairy tales."

"Oh, not really. I pick up my stories from real life."

The divine one gazes at me intensely for an instant. I think she's curious.

"I thought reality was uglier."

I light a cigarette and blow the smoke out forcefully.

"It is and it isn't. I know a lot of criminals."

She watches me in silence. Then decides, perhaps, to trust me.

"Ah! You know what? I'd like to meet a few criminals. Why don't you bring me along sometime?"

I look at her. Her eyes glow with excitement.

Alice and Alvise, who are sitting back at the table, don't seem to mind our lengthy absence.

I cast the blonde the predatory look of a black panther.

"If you ask me with those eyes, I'll take you all the way to hell!"

Dorothea laughs again. The night advances with a Greek profile and the fixed gaze of the sphinx. The feline night works for me.

Alice and the kids are leaving for California. A seaside vacation. Suitcases, bags and toys.

Yes, I confess, I am sending them away. Chucky, that smart kid, looks at me as if he understands everything.

"Getting rid of us, aren't you, Calagan?"

"It's better if I stay home alone."

Like a typical female, Chipper kisses me while snatching some money from my pockets.

The brigade marches out of the house noisily. I emphasize my crisis by following them with a pale, sickly smile.

"Old Calagan is tired."

Alice, wearing a close-fitting safari outfit, carefully scrutinizes my face.

"Oh, yeah, 'cause now it's all our fault that you're exhausted."

"What do you want from me? Don't go, then. I didn't ask you to leave."

"Oh, no. No, dear. We're leaving. Stay by yourself, do what you want. You're crazy if you think I'm going to believe that we're to blame for your nervous breakdown. What did the doctor say? You've got to have peace and be left alone, right? Well, great! Stay by yourself like some beast in its lair! I look forward to seeing the results. Fancy that! So long."

She gives me a cold kiss.

I kiss the children as they take off down the steps.

"Hey. Be careful now. 'Bye-bye."

Alice doesn't even turn around.

"You be careful."

I stand at the door and wave at them.

Well, if a casual bystander had happened to find himself in front of my garden that summer morning, he would have been able to see the enigmatic smile of contentment on my lips. Excuse me, casual bystander, if I slam the door in your face. I have things to do.

I run back inside and grab the phone. I already know the number by heart.

"Hello? Dorothea? Is that you?"

A group of buxom Puerto Rican women are dancing in front of a bar. All around, tough street kids shake their torero-asses to Afro-Hispanic rhythms. *Puertorico . . . Olé!* "Things are better in America . . . Americaaaa!"

We are in the heart of the Puerto Rican slums on the Lower East Side, a neglected area of Manhattan known as Alphabet Land, because of its lettered avenues. A neighborhood brimming with misery and color. It is one of the ghettos belonging to the bitter, marginal world of Old New York.

I am walking with Dorothea down one of these little streets. A "friend" takes us. The *amigo* is greasy, colorful, fat and mustached, and wears black sunglasses. His aura of poorly digested wealth suggests ill-gotten gains, and his cheap, flashy style is typical of a dubious *nouveau riche* on the way up the social ladder of ethnic minorities. In other words, that loud, eccentric vulgarity which first characterized the Chinese, Mexican and Italian underworld, and now, the black and Puerto Rican.

Some are able to rise from that sea of misery: ostentation, vulgarity, ignorance, Mafia prostitution, drugs and even worse. Indeed, our *amigo* is a "boss." He is Nacho "el Gordo," one of the many bosses and demi-bosses in the world of organized crime that flourishes in the barren soil of the Puerto Rican ghetto.

Nacho is flattered by my friendship, and I think of him as a valuable informer and a great source of son-of-a-bitch crime stories. This time, however, it is a special occasion.

Nacho el Gordo literally goes wild when he catches sight of the beautiful blond Italian countess.

Dorothea is dressed in white, and her blond hair is tossed by an occasional gust of wind. She reminds me of a young Englishwoman involved in a colonial romance, except that she also has Mediterranean curves and charm.

I devour her with my eyes as I act out the part of the "Mafioso" with Nacho el Gordo, who plays the godfather. He goes on talking and talking.

"Would you like something to drink?"

Dorothea gives me a dazzling smile.

"No, thank you. I am absolutely fascinated."

The streets are crowded with people. The smell of garlic fills the air. Someone beckons to Nacho el Gordo. The fat one excuses himself and takes off.

Dorothea and I stroll along the street as we wait for the Puerto Rican to return. I watch her out of the corner of my eye, mentally licking my lips.

Dammit! I like her. Yes, I can even devour her with my eyes. I really like her. She turns me on. Dorothea lights a cigarette and catches the glint of my eye. I'm feeling dizzy. Dorothea affects me like champagne. I am getting drunk on her.

"Why that smile? It makes you look like the Mona Lisa."

"Hm-mmmm . . ."

I heave a long, comic sigh which makes Dorothea laugh.

"Why are you sighing like that?"

"Why? Well, just because Alvise is a very old friend of mine. At least let me sigh. Hm-mmm. Yeah, okay. Because you see, if it wasn't for Alvise, I'd tell you what a sexy broad you are. I mean, you're such a knockout that if a guy loses his head and rapes you right in the middle of the street, well . . . they'd acquit him. It's too much! You're too beautiful. And is that the way to go around? In that flimsy silk shirt? It's a serious provocation. With you here, dressed like that, I just might get a healthy Puerto Rican knife between my shoulder blades. How could anyone not acquit the guy who rapes you? Oh,

you're so . . . not only gorgeous, but also . . . so . . . so
. . . sexy, exciting, thrilling, captivating, aphrodisiacal,
sensual, liquid, misty, silky, soft, firm, shapely, mysterious, erotic, feminine, equivocal, enchanting, exalting,
stupendous, magnificent . . ."

While I blurt these attributes, Dorothea begins to
laugh as if she were watching an acrobat walking across
a tightrope.

"That's enough. Stop it."

"Yes, I better . . ."

I pause and look into her eyes.

". . . because of Alvise."

Dorothea's laughter dies down. The fat Puerto Rican
comes back.

"Excuse me, *Señora.*"

We continue our walk down the little streets. The
crowd on stoops and corners is full of dark mustaches
and threatening macho eyes, strongly reacting to Dorothea's presence.

I try to protect her. If Nacho el Gordo weren't
around, things would get quite sticky.

Despite everything, I still sigh in her ear.

"Because of Alvise."

She looks off into the distance.

"Let's not talk about Alvise."

There is a slight tone to her voice that irritates me.

"Why not?"

"Because Alvise . . . is Alvise."

That pisses me off. I'm furious. What the fuck does
that mean? "Alvise is Alvise"? Dorothea walks on with
her loose, languid stride.

What can that mean—"Alvise is Alvise"? I mean, *who* is he? The sum of all perfections? Like Chinese porcelain?! Like Leslie Howard in *Gone With the Wind?!* If so, he must be boring as hell. Maybe that's what her tone meant. She can't take it anymore. Nobody could put up with such perfection. You end up getting desperate. Yeah, but she, on the other hand, is mysterious. She has shadowy corners, and deep hollows. And it is within those dark hollows that I place all my hopes.

We walk by a construction yard, full of workers. Dark eyebrows, enormous mustaches. Thick pectoral and underarm fur. From high above the scaffolding they yell things to Dorothea. The fat one casts threatening looks.

"*La señora es guapíssima. Aquí somos hombres apasionados. Perdóname, Señora.* The lady is very beautiful. Around here, the men are hot blooded. Excuse me, *Señora.*"

Dorothea smiles. Her nostrils flare. Something strange flashes in her golden eyes. She's excited. She feels the men's arousal swelling around her and inhales it deeply, as if it were a drug.

The men are growing restless. Some of them sing in a gypsylike fashion. They howl some ayayayayaaaa!

The fat one gets nervous and yells back at the workers. The men, electrified, react badly. Our little tour risks taking a bad turn.

In the midst of the screaming and confusion, I put my arm around Dorothea to protect her.

And I find myself close to her blond hair and rosy ear.

"Dorothea. Dorothea. Who are you? A cruel, lascivious leopard, hmmm? It looks as if you like this dirty, desperate lust. This air, thick with testosterone. Are you perhaps like one of those Roman matrons who wanted to make love with the gladiators before they got slaughtered in the arena? You know, if the fat one gets nervous, the whole thing might end in a knifing."

Dorothea smiles, but I can see her excitement is real.

"Then take me away. I'm ready to go. Tell me, where do they hold their black masses?"

Good. Everything is going according to plan. We come upon a small, abandoned port on the East River. Nacho el Gordo proudly shows us a derelict barge. On the side of the boat is a name which is as exciting as a Spanish gypsy guitar: *La Malagueña.*

The fat one introduces us to a dark little man who wears a gold gypsy ring in one ear.

"This is *el galeón del caribe.* Listen, Juan, Sammy is my brother. Watch where you put your feet, *Señora.* There, *mira.* You know, this used to be a trash barge."

With the expertise of an old sea dog, I hold my hand out to Dorothea and help her up the rickety gangplank. Then we enter the roomy belly of the boat.

Following the fat one's orders, the little man opens up a trapdoor. It's a sort of secret passage.

Nacho el Gordo's fleshy voice shakes his large stomach as he guides us through the boat.

"Here, *aquí, Señora. Mira al casco,* look at the bottom. *Es una bariga cargado de aventuras,* the belly of this boat is filled with adventures."

"Oh, really?"

"La Malagueña *ha visto los nacimientos y las muertes de muchas estrellas* . . . has seen the births and deaths of many stars. We called her the '*Malagueña* with the golden belly' after we'd been with her a year. Nice time it was back then. She's carried dreams along with millions of dollars in bottles of gin. Those were the glorious old days. *Ahora,* she's like a *mujer hermosa* in calmer waters. But she's still seductive. Back in 1933 . . ."

Well, he could go on talking for sixty hours straight. He could tell you the whole story of Prohibition since its beginning.

I make secret signs to the fat one to make himself scarce. Nacho el Gordo, as always, quick on the uptake, gives me a look of envy. Then, with a nod of his head and an ambiguous smile, he calls the man with the earring away with him.

I lead my blond goddess down below deck. There's a strong smell of mold, but the atmosphere is beautiful, mysterious, like a classic thriller—in other words, just what we needed.

Dorothea advances in the twilight. The low-ceilinged, ample space of the boat's belly is decorated with bizarre paintings: There are magic symbols, traces left from the Brazilian Condomblé rites, blue and white festoons, amulets, candles, shells, crosses, masks, black rooster feathers, horns, drums and other various painted animal-skin instruments.

The entire setup looks like it comes right out of the "Museo Antropológico Folklórico de los Hombres." In other words, the atmosphere of a witch doctor's hut.

Dorothea seems fascinated.

"This is fantastic. Is this the place where they hold the black masses?"

"That's right. Macumbas and Condomblé."

Nacho el Gordo waves at us from the trapdoor above.

"'Scuse me, Sammy, but I gotta run. Urgent business. Sorry. *Adios, Señora.*"

He tips his hat theatrically and disappears, followed by the man with the earring.

We are alone in that closed-in place. Together, mature adults.

Dorothea has a serene, childlike expression on her face. She looks around with interest. I arch my eyebrows in the style of Clark Gable, and attempt a "Rhett Butler" smile—remember *Gone With the Wind?*—experienced, ironic, irresistible. You can get this kind of smile by sucking in your cheeks and keeping them tight with your molars.

"Do you like it here?"

She gives me an amused look.

"What was that you whispered to me before? What am I? A lascivious leopard? You think I'm vicious and depraved, don't you?"

I suddenly catch my reflection in a dark mirror. My annoying self-critical alter ego begins its persecution.

"Scum. You're a pig . . . a stinking worm . . . a slimy bastard . . . Do you see anything kosher, civilized or admirable about enticing the wife of your old friend— maybe your *best* friend—so that you can placate your inferiority complex? You're doing it out of spite, and you even choose such kitschy methods. It's all a lot of cheap folklore, touristy crap. Do you really think you're a gentleman?"

I glance back at the mirror and mentally curse my image: "Ffffuckkofff!!!"

Then, with a rapid about-face and some sort of elegant tango step . . . Bammm!!!

I nonchalantly kick the pole that holds up the trapdoor. The cover comes down with a crash that echoes through the hollows of the barge. Dorothea gives a start. We are locked inside. The situation is under my control. I'll handle this like a gentleman.

"Oh, dammitall! The trapdoor fell. It must have slipped." Her eyes flash a strange green light.

"It might have something to do with the magic forces in this place. Don't you think?"

I stand still and look at her intensely. Slightly equivocal, ironic and certainly sexy.

"Afraid? I'll protect you. I've got a luminous aura, you know. Exù watches over me, and gives me powers."

Dorothea is near a set of bongos now, and begins beating out a Latin rhythm on them. She is damn good at it, just like a professional. She speaks in the same rhythm.

"So, why don't you do something for me, like perform a macumba, I don't know. Read my hand, or something like that."

The bitch is provoking me. And I increase the intensity of my mysterious, ironic gaze and become extremely sexy.

"Sure, I'll do a macumba for you. But goddammit, stop playing those bongos like that. They're driving me crazy. They're horribly sensual. I could . . . lose control . . ."

The Clark Gable-Rhett Butler act ended a while ago. Now, I choose from a more modern repertory, I seek inspiration in the contemporary. I mean old Brando: the eye cast over to the upper left-hand corner. And then, Jack Nicholson: extravagant, dissident, cross-eyed, irresistible and charming. The Last Lover, naturally. Hey, baby, how about a little snort? This stuff's top grade. "I can't give you anything but coke, baby . . ."

Dorothea looks at me maliciously.

"You could lose control, really? Come on! What a liar! I saw you close that trapdoor. And you know it."

She throws her head back, laughing. Then she stretches out on a bed full of strange cushions, with dolls and black feathers. The bed must have been used by the witch doctor when he performed his black masses and voodoo ceremonies. Witch doctors! What sons of bitches! Throw off the mask and they're almost always dirty old pigs.

She is beautiful, the seductive blonde—hips, tits and ass—the lady is a whore. Damn, she looks like a *Playboy* centerfold. I have a violent urge for intimacy.

"Witch."

"Son-of-a-bitch."

She laughs again. I look at her. *Ah! Go ahead and laugh, you hussy. I'll make you laugh now.*

I throw myself on top of her laugh. I silence it with strong hands and mouth. Even a bit brutal.

Dorothea has trouble breathing. Between kisses, she gasps for air like a drowning swimmer.

"Oh, God! What fire!"

"Ssssshhhh . . . Quiet!"

I slide my hand through her hair and pull her head back. One, two, three—the buttons pop off her blouse. And down we go! Hooked finger around her panties, obviously lace ones. Elementary, my dear Watson!

I'm playing the tough guy, but I'm gone. I begin to have trouble keeping up the Bogart voice. I mean, with the Gable smile, the Brando eyes and the Nicholson nostrils, things are becoming a mess.

There isn't any time for self-criticism however. I tug, and her panties come off in shreds.

"I'm checking out the merchandise, baby. Show me what you can do."

In the dark macumba mirror, my image reflects a violent and fantastic passion. The part of me that hates myself makes another of its eternal efforts to pull me down and destroy me, trying to add to my complexes:

"What a scene. You're really going through the whole repertory. Including the *Kamasutra*. Who do you think you are? Superman? What's going on inside your mind while you pump away like a horny bull, like a debt-ridden Latin lover with a millionairess? What are you thinking about? Hmm? That Alvise is too much of a poet to be a good stud? Of course. You consider yourself a super-endowed macho hunk of man. How did it go? Didn't you use to steal the girls from the six-foot-tall blond tennis champions who looked like Robert Redford? Didn't you always drive Alice's friends crazy with your legendary sex performances? You were talked about, weren't you? All the girls talked to their friends, curlers in their hair and polish on their toenails, didn't they? And the legend became a myth. What is that beast you have between your legs? A jaguar? A bison? A boa? An elephant? An orangutan? Poor megalomaniac. Tell the truth: You hope yours is bigger than Alvise's! Just like the old Italian joke about 'Alfonso's widow.' The brokenhearted, faithful widow, after many years finally succumbs to a lover. After their first night of lovemaking, she goes over to the portrait of her dear, departed husband and says: 'Alfonso, take this,' and blows her hubby a Bronx cheer, in memory of his lousy performances.

"There. That's exactly what your dream is. You overwhelm, overturn and sweep her away with your power and your sadistic refinement of a great lover, hoping that she'll go back and blow a Bronx cheer in Alvise's face! You're vulgar and pathetic! But all the same, I've got to admit you've got endurance going for you. Who could ever imagine that envy would produce such aphrodisiac powers? Hey, you still at it? It's incredible. Watch out, you son-of-a-bitch. You're skating dangerously along the edge of a heart attack. You're not a kid anymore. You're about to kick the bucket. Wowww, there it goes. Sweet Jesus, I told you so . . . It's a heart attack!"

No! I only collapse, utterly exhausted after my great performance. In my sweaty, comatose state, I manage to get a glimpse of Dorothea, beautiful and classy as usual, despite her nudity, her matted hair and runny mascara. However, I obviously ravaged her. Her low, velvety, sexy voice caresses my ear with a murmur.

"*C* minus."

What? What? What did she say? Am I mistaken or did she whisper "C minus"?

"What do you mean, C minus?"

Dorothea arches her eyebrows a bit, and a flash of animation filters sleepily through her eyelashes.

"On the traditional American grading system, A plus through F naturally."

My persecuting, ball-breaking superego sneers at me from within.

"Did you hear her, you scum? Now you really look like shit!"

I am deeply offended. My incredible wrath gives me superhuman strength and a stroke of energy. Drugs, angel dust and magic mushrooms may do the trick, but there's nothing like someone knocking your style to give you an extra charge. I inspire fear. I get up like a bull.

"C minus for me? C minus?! I'll show you a C minus!"

I throw myself back down on the blond goddess. I'm pissed as hell, and my rage gives me a titanic force.

It's so true. Hatred can do more than love. In fact, she thinks I am making love, but I am actually making hate! A double somersault, enough to destroy a buffalo.

I am like an Olympic champion during his final effort. I am purple, with my muscles contracted. My veins and tendons are bulging like tree roots. My body is perfectly arched as I perform the act for the third outstanding time. Incredible! My chest is shaken by the primitive howling of a caveman.

I suddenly collapse with a crash.

Incredible, isn't it? I did it! Yeah!

Time slides wearily over our sweaty, prostrate bodies. Dorothea is really wiped out this time. She lies there in total abandon, relaxed, superbly beautiful and a little sad.

I, on the other hand, feel like a dirty, wet towel thrown on the bathroom floor of a fourth-class hotel.

Dorothea begins to mumble some sort of confession. I listen, exhausted.

"Vietnam, Ché Guevara, Mao. Then I got into a real emotional mess over Cambodia. Things only got worse with Pol Pot. That whole business of genocide. The last shock was the Arab world—Iran. A group of us went there to give our support to the women's struggle against repression. You know, when they reimposed the veil and the execution of adulteresses. Then the whole business with the hostages started. I offered myself, but you can imagine . . . They didn't want me. They put me on a plane immediately and sent me to London."

She keeps talking and talking. My persecuting superego begins to tease me again.

"Ha, ha, ha, ha. She's a real neurotic like all intellectual high-class phoenixes. Poor thing. She comes to you to unleash all her political and ideological frustrations. She doesn't know you couldn't give a fuck about all that! She doesn't even suspect what a pathetic creature you really are. Or perhaps she does, and she's only talking to herself, as if she were alone.

No, it is not true. She *is* talking to me. After all, I am an intellectual too! And I have to prove it to myself immediately. I attack!

"You're telling me. Jesus! I've gone through all those classic stages too. Shitheads. We committed intellectuals have always been shitheads. We don't even know what not to believe in anymore. The few ideas we have are confused. You take pains to understand, but in the end you understand nothing. Marx, Engels, China, Trotsky, Eurocommunism, the new philosophers. We turned a blind eye on everyone, even Khomeini. We all believed in a sacrosanct struggle for freedom and a revolt of the people. The Ayatollah once seemed enlightened and progressive, with a tendency toward socialism."

I light a cigarette, trying to act nonchalant. I swear to myself that I won't remove the cigarette from my mouth! I have to make an ash an inch long—you know, like Gabin in *Quai des Brumes* or Montand in *Z*. After all, the intellectuals, and I mean the serious ones—those who've got ashes on their jacket lapels—all live in Europe, and usually end up in Paris.

"And now just take a look at the rift in the great ideology of the Left—with its state of crisis, the conflicts within parties, and widespread terrorism. And Poland with Solidarity."

Dorothea looks at me.

"Don't tell me, you're a Com . . ."

I cut her off with a kiss. When our lips part, she continues.

". . . munist!"

"No."

"Radical chic?"

"Radical shit. I was interested in communism when it seemed like a mortal sin and Stalin was the devil. But then began the collective sale of the soul in exchange for television. It has lost all its charm."

Dorothea laughs. I go on with it. I remember having read certain phrases in an Italian newspaper, and I have even written them down somewhere. Now is my chance to use them.

" 'The people' are no more, only the public remains. Eliot said: 'This is the way the world ends, not with a bang, but a whimper.' I fear it may end more pathetically with 'Ladies and Gentlemen, the party's over'!"

A long ash on the end of my cigarette. I pause as Bogart would have done, and then get down to business.

"And Alvise?"

The ash falls on my jacket lapel.

Dorothea pretends not to hear.

I take the cigarette out of my mouth. I turn around, I kiss her and try again:

"Alvise?"

Dorothea stiffens a bit.

"What about Alvise?"

I look off into the distance. Light years away, other times, other memories. I sigh and blow out the smoke.

"I feel like a bastard. You can't understand. Alvise is a friend. It's your fault. No, I'm not joking anymore. You're too beautiful. You're a serious provocation. All the penal codes provide for extenuating circumstances."

"Stupid."

"Do you love Alvise?"

Dorothea doesn't answer me. She turns around and listlessly lights a cigarette.

"Let's not talk about Alvise."

I'm getting nervous.

"No, let's *do* talk about him. Alvise is more than a brother to me. This is serious. You, why did you do it? A whim? Or maybe you're not getting on well with Alvise?"

My ball-breaking conscience criticizes me harshly:

"You're really screwing things up. You're a worthless creep. A disaster. Why don't you learn? Learn from her. Look at her class, her discretion."

Dorothea exhales the smoke like Dietrich in the style of the marvelous thirties. She takes her time before answering.

"What does Alvise have to do with anything? Let's leave him out of this. Please."

I feel bad but I insist.

"No, I'm sorry. I have to know. Do you love Alvise?"

"What kind of question is that? Alvise . . . Alvise."

Now her eyes float away among the stars. Who knows where she is flying to? There is something glowing in her upcast eyes. She sighs.

"Alvise is different. We have a special relationship. Sorry, I don't know how to explain it. It's something only the two of us understand."

I'm getting incredibly nervous and have trouble controlling myself. But I manage to feign indifference.

"Do you love him?"

I was messing everything up. I could feel it.

I am stupid and vulgar, while she remains untouchable and enigmatic like an egg. A true lady. Very, very, very irritating. She looks at me smugly.

Then she takes off again on one of her flights. She speaks softly and slowly, in a demure tone.

"He's the most extraordinary person I've ever met in my life. He's marvelous, don't you agree?"

"Huh? Yes... No. I don't know. But, then... I mean, why are you here with me? You talk about him with so much love. Help me to understand. What is he to you? Is he your guru? Your political leader? Your god? Shit! Why are you here with me, huh?"

Dorothea stares at me with her transparent eyes, which this time are precisely like a Magritte painting. Behind them are blue skies with floating clouds, little birds, lines of poetry, breezes and dead leaves.

"You want to label everything. What a bore! What do the reasons matter? Think what you want—that I'm a nymphomaniac, that I'm depraved, spoiled. Do you think it really matters?"

I couldn't take it anymore. Very, very irritating.

"Don't speak to me as if I were retarded! What if I fall in love with you? I'm no good. It could end up badly. That's why I have to know."

A delightful little smile appears on her face.

"You're cute and you're also a liar. You know what we'll do, sweetheart? Anything you want. We'll see each other. We won't see each other. As you like."

We are driving back toward Manhattan.

Dorothea's beautiful hair blowing in the wind, indifferently. I drive, straining to control my tics.

I am a disaster. I do not understand anything. Maybe she's making fun of me, I feel ridiculous.

My pain-in-the-ass superego begins to taunt me again:

"You deserve it, you little vindictive worm. It was all just a whim of hers. That's it. You don't even dare to ask her if she's dumping you or if she plans on seeing you again."

I look at myself in the rearview mirror and then glance through the corner of my eye at the mysterious goddess by my side. One thing is certain: I haven't touched Alvise with this whole dirty story, not even with a fingernail.

I am back in my study at my desk in the throes of another identity crisis. The only sign of movement is the constant twitching of my tics.

I look at myself in the mirror. I hate myself. Yeah, worms are feeding on me, and a demon is tormenting me.

It's true. I'm not at all happy about having gone to bed with Alvise's wife. In fact, things seem even worse than before. Dorothea is completely unruffled. She said Alvise is divine. And me?!!! Me? Well, as for me—instead of feeling like a macho superstud, I feel used and tacky. A fart in a hurricane. Even worse: as if she had taken advantage of my identity crisis to rob me of my strength and my sex, and screw me up. No, now I am really cracking up. No. Now I'll call her and . . .

Destiny really has a sense of timing. The telephone rings.

"Hello?"

It's Alvise.

"Is that you, Alvise? How strange. I was just about to call you, but you called me instead. You wouldn't be reading my mind, would you? Hmm? Oh, I'm fine, just fine. I'm better. I feel lousy. No, honestly. I really don't feel like going out at all. I'm not going out. I don't feel like it. No. Yes. All right, I'm coming. Where?"

I hang up.

My private persecutor scoffs at me:

"See? You told him you weren't going out! Instead, you end up going. See? You're an inferior being. As soon as he opens his mouth, you turn to jelly. You pull your pants down. Look at yourself. An inferior being winding around the spiral of his inferiority. That's what you are. You wanted to splash mud on him, and instead you're the one who's covered with it, you're drowning in it, closer and closer to the bottom."

I turn on my superego like a tiger. I look in the mirror for my persecuting image:

"Listen, you asshole. No, it's not true! Maybe I made a mistake. But you'll see! I'll raze that colossus with clay feet. I'll have that divine Alvise bite the dust at my feet. And over his ruins, I shall erect the monument of my new self."

"Oh, really? And where do you have to meet him now? At an exhibit of gestural art? What kind of crap is that?"

"How do I know?"

"Hey, watch out. It's cultural stuff. He'll outdo you there. He'll screw you there!"

"Go fuck yourself, okay?"

Projected lights. Exhibition of gestural art. A pregnant woman with worms on her belly, disgusting. A very selective public of intellectuals and artists. Serious and deep comments. It's a "historical" exhibit, the art of the last twenty years.

Critics and painters are debating the subject as if it belonged to the remote past! Conceptual art, behavioral art, land art, minimal art, body art, hyperrealism and other "isms" I'd never heard of before.

Alvise speaks with them about contemporary painting, which is attempting a return to canvasses and brushes. I try to appear knowledgeable on the subject, but I'm completely lost. Bewildered, I look at a box on which is printed: "The artist's shit." Then I glance at a wall on which someone has written, "Art is dead."

Alvise goes on talking about the art of the past twenty years. Everyone listens to him with awe. The artists surround him. Andy Warhol tries to kiss his hand. Rauschenberg listens to him with closed eyes. Segal asks for his autograph. They obviously look up to him as a great authority. I'm green. I feel like a turd. I strongly suspect that Alvise's faking and that it's all bullshit. I'm foaming at the mouth. I stare at him.

I suddenly superimpose on his image the painting of Salome—the one from the Villa Ombreggiata in Venice. It is a very distinct picture in my mind. Immediately, Strauss's music fills the air! And a sort of ballet, worthy of La Scala, is performed in my head.

Alvise's severed head lies on a silver platter. I'm dressed in Salome's veils as I dance for the tetrarch in the hope of obtaining the prophet's head.

The music grows louder.

It is evening now, and Alvise has brought me back to his house for a drink.

His house is a jewel. Outside there is a sort of jungle, which is visible from the big window. Lianas, baobabs, palm trees. I'm waiting for Tarzan to show up, with tigers and King Kong, among the leaves.

"That's quite a jungle you've got out there, and to think it's right in the heart of Manhattan."

"Oh, it's just a hidden corner of Gramercy Park. Why don't you have a seat?"

Alvise sits down in a leather armchair. The color of the leather is superb.

"Ah! Does this color leather exist? I thought it only appeared in English movies and in interior decorating magazines. Snazzy stuff here. Well, you've got a lot of class. Congratulations. This place must have cost you quite a bundle."

"Oh, no. It's not mine. It belongs to a friend. He's away and has kindly let us stay here. One shouldn't have houses, my dear Sammy. They become traps, even tombs."

"Well, you can afford not to have any, because you've got a friend who can lend you one. But if he didn't have one, and neither did anyone else, we might just be having a drink up in a tree now."

"And wouldn't that be lovely? Come here. Come on. What's wrong? Hmmm? Spill out your troubles to an old childhood friend. What is it?"

He smiles at me affectionately, which gets on my nerves. It is clear that he cares about me. I confess that there is something in his eyes that makes me want to lay my head on his shoulder. Boy, am I an asshole.

I dawdle. I affect indifference and superiority. Then, dammitall, I begin to talk. I let it all out. I'm scared. I'll end up pulling my pants down.

"These thrillers! I hate them. I can't stand them anymore. I wasn't made to write that crap. I . . . You don't know this, but at college they bet on me. I used to write well. I was also very involved in politics. But I threw it all away like a *schmuck.* "

There. I knew it. I open up. It all gushes forth. I pour out my anxieties on my friend's chest. Off with the pants. Boy, am I really an asshole! I can't stop talking.

"A third-rate intellectual sold for two cents. I . . . I . . . I don't know why I'm telling you all this stuff. I feel overwhelmed. Some verbal form of diarrhea has taken hold of me! I can't control myself. I once had an idea, a great idea. About a book. An idea . . . I mean, the worst thing that can happen to a genius is to be understood, right?"

By now I'm babbling on incessantly, worse than an analysand. He listens to me with sympathetic eyes.

"Something that begins with this concept: that beyond divine providence, there has to be a divine *im*providence in the world. Involving everything. Okay? And we, who write—I mean, who are we writing for? Are we writing for the masses? I mean, you can't become their slaves and you can't abandon them either. An intellectual should think, shouldn't he? Of course, the masses surround him like a pack of hungry tigers, blind and suicidal. The masses who eat everything, buy everything, vomit everything, digest everything and defecate everything—all by way of words. An ocean of words. The idea was: *Project for a world without words.* You see,

I really wanted the title to be *No!* But then I was afraid. Please don't look at me so intently, as if I were Thomas Mann or Kafka visiting Victor Hugo. You're making me nervous."

Alvise gives me a little smile, then says to me:

"Don't you think they went through these moments too? On the contrary, all of us have that right. It's not only a duty, but also a vital necessity. I have an enormous respect for your literary work. Your mysteries are brilliant. But in some way, it does seem that you're betraying your true self. Sammy, you are a poet."

His eyes are sparkling at me.

"Yes, your true nature is simple and vital, and it lies buried deep within you. Our terrible yet marvelous childhood had a great effect on us. You stayed here, in America. What I'm trying to say is, remember that center for Jewish refugee children, where people came to adopt us, the poor little orphans? That's when the blockage occurred. I don't know how it happened, but I lost you there. And God knows how much time I spent looking for you. I waited there for hours on end with that gentleman who'd come to take me away. It was as if you'd disappeared into thin air. Where were you? Had you fallen asleep behind a couch? When I went back the next day, it was too late. You had already left with your new adoptive parents, and it was against the rules for them to give out addresses unless you were a close relative. Otherwise, I would have brought you to Italy with me and you would have gone on to study the classics in Verona. In other words, you would have had a different impact. You see, culture here, in this enormous country, is always struggling with the state religion—The Almighty Dollar. Faith in money and success is a cult that confuses ideas. But fortunately, poetry is still in you, smoldering under the ashes, and you've just realized that. The ashes of your success haven't put out the fire. Thank God! Your crisis is simply the need to express yourself. Now, it's your right, your duty and also a vital need: You have an urge to sing. With all the respect I have for mysteries and commercial literature, I still feel that you ought to allow yourself this one opportunity. Treat yourself to this luxury. Trust yourself. Bet on yourself. Only think about things you like! Write. Take all the time you want—without any obligation to your wife, children or anything else. Your first debt is always to yourself."

He is a guardian angel. Affection, respect. That concerned tone and sweet look of his gets on my nerves! I'd prefer anything else. Benevolence irritates me and saps me of my strength! The more he proves how good and perfect he is, the weaker I become and the more my hatred for him grows. An irresistible, demoniacal desire suddenly flashes through my mind. Something that might wipe that kind, protective expression right off his face. Something to disrupt that harmony inside him.

"I can't accept this help from you, Alvise. Because I committed a sin against you."

Sin—what a dumb choice of words. Anyway, Alvise raises one of his beautiful tapered hands.

"Who doesn't commit sins against others? Look, just forget it."

Hell, no! I was going to make sure he felt the blow. I wasn't going to let the matter drop.

"But I have to talk to you about it. You don't know . . ."

He interrupted me again.

"Are you sure it's a good idea to talk? Certain things are better left unsaid. Believe me."

Holy shit! Why is he carrying on like this? Why does he say that? Maybe he suspects. Maybe he is afraid. Maybe underneath that kind smile of his, he too is going through hell. He suspects, but doesn't want to know. Yes. That must be it. He doesn't want to suffer.

Fancy that!! I did it on purpose! Don't delude yourself that I'm not gonna tell you. From this moment on, your peace of mind is over, Alvise. From this moment on, you'll be tortured by the thought of my hands having touched your wife's body.

> What sense had I of her stol'n hours of lust?
> I saw it not, I thought it not, it harm'd not me;
> I slept the next night well, fed well, was free and
> merry;
> I found not Cassio's kisses on her lips.
> He that is robb'd, not wanting what is stol'n,
> Let him not know't, and he's not robb'd at all.

Othello, or rather good old Will, who's an expert on human feelings, is so right. No way. Now you'll have to hear the tragic truth. You've been robbed and you have to know it. I will tell you, you will hate me and at least we'll be even.

"I'm sorry, Alvise, but I just can't stay silent."

"As you wish, Sammy. If you think it will help you."

Yes, it will help me, dear super-perfect, superior being. It will help me to watch you turn pale, watch everything slide out from underneath you, watch you writhe in pain and watch your hatred gradually color your benevolent gaze a nasty shade of green.

"I've been to bed with Dorothea."

Alvise looks down. He doesn't turn a hair. He seems made of alabaster.

"Yes, I know."

He knows?! Why does he know? What does he know? How the hell does he know? What the fucking shit is he saying?!

"You know? You know? But how do you know? What do you know? Why do you know?"

"Dorothea told me."

He raises two kind, clear, innocent eyes. I feel like shit.

"She told you?"

"Yes. It might seem strange to you, maybe, but between us . . ."

He gets up and calmly straightens a painting.

"We have a profound, special relationship. I really love Dorothea. And one cannot love a person without accepting him or her entirely. I love Dorothea as she is. She's an extraordinary human being, you know. She has such courage, such sensitivity."

Speak of the devil! Who should have opened the door just then but the dazzling, ethereal Dorothea. Her eyes cut out of blue spring skies.

"How are you, darling? Was the exhibit any good?"

She kisses Alvise.

He looks at her lovingly. I am the only one who feels embarrassed. My image, reflected in the window pane at the end of the room, wears a grimace. My ball-busting alter ego breaks loose and torments me:

"You're annihilated, destroyed, kaput. You're nothing but a wounded, wriggling worm. The worm is incapable of understanding how two superior beings can go on talking peacefully, despite the fact that only a few hours ago the lady was having her buttocks and pubis slammed by your notorious beast, your orangutan. You're just a sleazy bastard who's eaten away with envy. An inferior being. Don't rack your brains to understand their superior breeding. It's beyond your comprehension!"

Alvise smiles at me.

Then he caresses Dorothea with a loving glance as she hands him a drink of something on the rocks.

She gazes back at him. Damn, damn, damn.

Yes! It would even be evident to a blind man. Those two love each other.

Yes, it's love—that special feeling that can put twinkling stars even in Hitler's eyes. That marvelous, celebrated sentiment that brings wings to the crippled, voices to the mute and a booming business to the card and chocolate companies on Valentine's Day. Love. Dammitall!

All right! Let's be reasonable. Above all, let's avoid paranoia. They love each other, and despite their love, she came to me, to get her valves greased by that vulgar Mike Bullit.

How do you explain that?

Maybe a whore? "Think what you want," that bitch of a blond goddess said. But what am I supposed to think, with those two looking at each other that way?

He squeezes her hand as he takes the glass, steamed with ice. There is an intense light in his eyes as he looks at her, like Gérard Philippe in *Le Diable au Corps* after the run through the rainstorm. That passionate, adolescent appeal. And combined, as usual, with the charm of the great heroes: Bogart in *Casablanca*, Cooper in *For Whom the Bell Tolls*, Howard in *Gone With the Wind*. Only that he is better than all of them, dammit. He's got more class.

Dorothea is drowning in his eyes.

Like a Stradivarius, he intones:

"How are you?"

Dorothea closes her eyes, nodding with the feline grace of a convalescent from a deathly illness.

"Fine."

And the suspicion comes to me that screwing must really be an illness for her. I don't know. It seems a bit like those relationships where one has a child under smack, or other heavy drugs. A good kid who seems straight, until he hits cold turkey. Withdrawal. Scandal. In other words, everything changes. God help us. I mean, if one evening the kid comes home full of booze, Mommy and Daddy throw a thanksgiving party for the miraculous event. I mean, everything is relative. Insofar as delirium tremens with consequent hallucinations of cockroaches and pink elephants is a joke for a parent, compared to a heroin overdose shot up with a Bic pen in a shitty latrine. Don't you agree? That is, my impression here is that he accepts her getting laid as if it were a drag on a cigarette. In other words: Dorothea-Alvise-love-cuckoldry, there's got to be something behind it.

Perhaps I'm wrong. Perhaps it's just a matter of superior culture.

It's not that I have hazy ideas about the concept of open marriage. That has nothing to do with it. Two people who are married love and respect each other, but they have their own separate lives. I can understand that.

From the very first day, I made it clear to Alice that if I ever caught her fooling around with someone else, I'd kick her out of the house, because I frankly don't give a shit about open marriage.

Just like I don't give a shit about all those other phony "liberated lifestyles"—*ménages à trois*, orgies and couples in quartets and sextets. Just props and excuses for the impotent. Alice, who is one of the more frequent beneficiaries of my roaring orangutan, knows very well that I don't need any of those dirty games to excite me. And if I want any extracurricular activity, I'll keep it away from my home and hearth. No problem—I can pick and choose.

But, let me make this perfectly clear, I want my wife clean, period.

So, getting back to the concept of open marriage, I can understand it, but several things in this particular case don't make any sense.

The couple in an open marriage do not sit around and share their experiences. They act nonchalant about the whole thing—as if nothing had happened, just like two old pals.

Here, instead, she tricked me, the blond sphinx, that hot piece of ice, because she went straight to him and spilled the beans, as if he were her analyst.

And then, all this love in their eyes. I don't have hang-ups about my body. The slight detail that Alvise is tall and handsome certainly hasn't affected me or cramped my style in any way. But the glowing love in their eyes is beyond comprehension.

Could she have done it to make him jealous? For godsake! Jealous? Him? Just imagine that perfect piece of Chinese porcelain jealous! No. Saints don't suffer from jealousy.

They are both so deeply involved in each other's eyes that I actually begin to feel like a fifth wheel. Could anyone have such shitty luck? And yet, that slutty phoenix liked our humping session, dammitall. I had her moaning.

I am sweating. I can see that they are passionately loving each other in front of my eyes. Maybe I'm going crazy.

Alvise turns his eyes away from her and smiles at me.

"You know, Dorothea, our Sammy's making a wise decision. He's returning to his true nature—poetry."

No, no, dear Mr. Holier-than-thou Alvise. No! You and your sweet paternal smile. "You're a poet. Drop everything. I'll stand by you." No! I don't want your help—you fucking Nobel Prize winner, helping your poor, underdeveloped friend! Forget it! I won't give you the satisfaction of becoming the recipient of your *noblesse oblige*, you cute, aristocratic little turd!

* * *

I'm in my study, talking to myself. I really look crazy, I know, because my persecuting alter ego, as usual, puts me on trial:

"Yours is a classic reaction among those who are inferior beings. Why don't you accept your status as a mediocre genius of the mass media? Otherwise, you're going to wind up with an ulcer."

The doorbell rings.

It is Billy O'Connor, the right-hand man of all tax-evaders. A neurotic little man who looks like a Hollywood bookmaker character of the thirties.

"Billy!"

He snickers and triumphantly brandishes a folder of documents. He casts a suspicious look toward the door and then whispers excitedly.

"Hold on to this stu-u-uff! Here's your man, Alvise Ottolenghi Portaleoni, a-a-alias Isaac Smith, now a stateless Jew."

He stammers out his vowels when he gets excited. After bleating for a while, he gets down to business.

"Born in Ferra-a-ara in 1930, to a wealthy Jewish family owning la-a-and, banks and real estate. He was left sole heir in 1948."

"Ah."

"He renounces it all on beha-a-alf of a foundation for former deported political prisoners, orphans and survivors of the concentration camps."

"What?"

"Yeah! Cra-a-azy! Never heard of anything of the kind before! Listen. He joins the Red Cross during the first A-a-arab-Israeli war, and becomes one of its dir-eectors at the end of the conflict. He sets up a kibbutz on the border, and gets a degree in philosophy and theology at the same time. Bu-u-ut when they offer him a post at the University of Tel A-a-aviv, he turns it down because he begins to disagree with the government's policies. He sta-a-arts a series of publications against the war and the hawks. He is a-a-alienated. Then he leaves for Asia. We know little about the time he spends in a Buddhist monastery there. Then he sets u-u-up a leper clinic. Ya getting the gist of it? And it's only the beginning. We find him later in the Bertrand Russell court in 1960, fighting against the atrocities of the Vietna-a-am War. In 1965, he leads a demonstration in favor of peace and civil rights in Berkeley. He stands by Ma-a-artin Luther King, Jr., during the long march. He tries to organize a protest in Moscow's Red Square for the dissidents and politica-a-al prisoners."

He goes on for another half-hour, telling me things that are out of this world—how Alvise trotted around the globe campaigning for peace, justice, nonviolence and civil rights! Stuff worth three covers on *Time* along with Superman and Mandrake. Billy's voice has grown hoarse by the time he reaches the final lap.

"A year ago, he obtains the Nobel Prize with a book of poetry. Tha-a-at wasn't enough! He gives up the royalties and everything on behalf of A-a-amnesty International. Now it seems he's the only person who can maintain any relations with the East, especially the Middle. Yeah, I forgot to tell you that he's also an expert on Eastern religions and a specialist in the Islamic faith. He got a degree from the Sorbonne in Kora-a-anic studies of the last Ayatollahs! He even knows Khomeini. The White House called upon him when we had the hostage crisis. The Aya-a-atollah preferred dealing with him instead of the UN. A-a-anyway, I told you that this stuff is simply unheard of. Never came across anyone like that in all my thirty years at the job. Even the guys down at the Lynx Detective A-a-agency said so. Hey, what's wrong? You look pale."

I'm wiping a bit of spittle from the corner of my mouth.

"Nothing, nothing. I'm fine."

I've lost control of my facial muscles. It takes me another half-hour, after Billy's departure, to get a hold of myself. I only feel better when I sense the shadow of a tranquilizing thought developing in the dark recesses of my suffering mind: I'll kill him.

I shudder and feel a little nauseous.

Perhaps I'm losing my marbles.

Perhaps . . . Could it be? That I really want to kill Alvise?

This sudden thought lights up in my brain. The words are written in neon, flashing lights and fireworks, with stars and sparks shooting up into the black sky of a summer evening.

"I must have Alvise's head."

Everything comes back to me in a flash. After all, who am *I?* I am a consumer, a contributor, a client, a club member, a current-account holder and a buyer. I am what I own—television set, cars, bank accounts, refrigerator and cashmere sweaters. I have a lot of things. I have a lot, therefore I am little. The degrading awareness of this fact struck me when I met *him*—Alvise. Alvise who has nothing, but who is. Alvise is a superior being. He made me feel inferior, precisely because he is superior. Yes, he is a real man! But, if he is a man, I am obviously a piece of shit. Therefore, in order to become a man myself, I first must kill him, the living proof of my inferiority. Am I clear? To all this should be added that mockery of my affair with Dorothea. The wife, the marvelous blond sphinx who—modestly—the orangutan, the stud, the bull, the "much-talked-about," the banging hammer, the super-endowed of the undersigned ... Sure, because you shouldn't forget that in college I used to steal the girls away from the six-foot-tall Robert Redford-type tennis champions, I've got witnesses, you can even ask my wife's friends ... As I was saying, the blond sphinx, the admirable phoenix, who was dragged through the feverish alcoves of sin and vice by the imposing, erogenous apparatus piloted by the undersigned—vigorously banging her for an absolutely exceptional number of times—and the blond sphinx liked it, and how! Well, as if nothing had happened ... period. I'll explain. I mean, in other words, nothing. Nothing at all. And you know why? Alvise is marvelous—she tells me. She's madly in love with him. Then why are you banging away with me, I ask? I say that ... that ... If I'm allowed a touch of vulgarity, we went through the whole repertory that could be found in the *Kamasutra,* Parisian brothels and Japanese porno prints. Every position. Right side up. Upside down. What does it mean? Is she a whore?

At this point, poor Sammy goes to Alvise and says: "Look, pal, sorry, but it happened—I mean, I *shtupped*

Dorothea, yeah, *Kamasutra*, brothels, the whole business." What would anyone expect? At least Alvise should turn pale and collapse, bursting into tears, I guess. "Poor me, she's the burden of my life," or else, "That woman is the devil, but I am a slave to love," or even "She's ill, a nymphomaniac, desperate," or something. What can I say: that he jumps on my throat, kicks me out of the house ... In brief, I should see him in difficulty, dammit, don't you think?

But no! Instead, he says: "Dorothea is marvelous, she's an extraordinary human being." Yeah, even better than Spencer Tracy and Katharine Hepburn. And you can't make heads or tails of it. It's enough to drive anyone crazy. And you can tell by the way they look at each other that they're in love, that they also get it on, that their marriage flows along smoothly.

Well, no! Because that way, I feel like a two-bit whore that she just used for kicks. Me, on the verge of a heart attack, after doing my best to the last drop of strength to impress her, a performance worthy of applause ... Well, can you believe it? The bitch—got that tone?—acted as though she'd eaten a potato chip, a cocktail olive, nothing more. And me a worm ... and them superior, and so, nothing. Me destroyed, and him unscathed.

Human blood flows in my veins. My murderous dreams about Alvise Ottolenghi Portaleoni are vital. I'm forced toward this murder because of higher powers or, rather, out of self-defense. In order to survive and remedy my nothingness, I must, first of all, eliminate him. On his ruins would rise a new man. The base of some new society. To be, I must have Alvise's head. I need, expect, I want Alvise's head.

I put my hand over my stomach. A sharp claw is clutching at my guts.

It's my ulcer! I finally understand why my stomach has remained calm up till now. It's only preparing a major attack. However, inside me a lamp is lit, within the dark recesses of the black well of evil intent. It's all clear to me. Now I know what to do! If I want to become a true artist, *I have to kill Alvise!*

It certainly helps to get things straight in your mind! I am at my desk, working with full efficiency, after so long.

I have my notebook, my reference books, my book-marks, a nice steaming cup of coffee and the best-stocked criminal library existing on Manhattan's East Side.

Well, first of all: classification, organization, planification.

"Poisons: curare. Concealment technique: few drops in an ice cube. An ice arrow. Instant death."

I take note of the curare ice arrow, change the book and go on with the list.

"Cyanide. Tastes like almonds. Concealment technique: injectable in a tube of almond-flavored toothpaste."

I place the book on the poisons pile and continue.

"Tetanus. Concealment technique: a rusted nail."

I go on to the next book.

"Can I come in?"

My heart skips a beat. I see Dorothea standing before me like one of my visions. I am petrified. The surprise gives me no pleasure. What can she want here, now?

Dorothea comes toward me, her long, shapely legs peeping through a barbaric violet-golden dress made of mirrors and jewels studded in a sea of veils from *A Thousand and One Nights*.

"I don't feel like sleeping tonight. Your door was open. Am I interrupting anything? I had a terrible meal with some boring Japanese sociologists."

She stretches out over the guanaco skin which lies on the sofa. Damn: The broad is gorgeous! Dammitall! Despite the fact that my vital interests are buried elsewhere, something inside me, like a conditioned reflex, makes me wobble over to those long, fantastic legs.

The orangutan feels like renewing its knowledge of her, in the biblical sense. It is growing restless and rapacious.

Dorothea begins talking. She is a real pain in the ass with her civil, political and social commitments. International human rights and all that jazz. She was like the front page of the Sunday *Times*. Yeah, yeah, her commitments! She might be superior, she might be anything, but tonight she is feeling horny and the little bitch has come to me to dance a tango.

She goes on talking about student movements around the world—the young Japanese Maoists and those Iranian Islamic students who are connected with Palestinian terrorism and in contact with Libya. She babbles on with her political bullshit, but her eyes really seem to say: "Come on, dummy, what are you waiting for? Hop on, let's go for a ride."

Okay, all right, the superstud is here, willing to offer his services, but at least the aching cluster of my frustrations would like to be soothed with some flattery! Yes, I want encomiums, tributes and homages.

I kneel down at the feet of that beautiful, infuriating divinity and try to re-create Al Capone's overwhelming virility, hoarse voice and mean look. Let's say De Niro in one of Scorsese's films, realism about New York's ethnic minorities, but in revolt.

I light a cigarette.

"Loosen up with the Japanese terrorism crap. Come on, admit it. You're here because you have the hots for me."

Dorothea responds with a silvery laugh. She nimbly grabs my neck with her feet in some sort of Judo maneuver. She has my head stuck between her knees in a stupid, humiliating position.

Then the goddess speaks with a sweet voice.

"Stupid, I was going to shoot myself tonight."

Now she is suddenly simple and serious, and you can tell she means what she says.

There, she's managed to bewilder me once again—shit! I sense there is some truth to her words. But what if she's teasing me? Uh-oh, wait a minute, the orangutan is letting loose. At this point, I don't give a damn about anything at all, and I let myself go.

I overwhelm her in a bout of savage lovemaking. It is violent, primitive and erotic.

I perform the orangutan's favorite variety of configurations: the Taming of the Wild Stallion; Sacrificial Rites in an Indian Temple; Phallophoria with Adoration; Love Knot—Sailor Style; Slaughter of the Bull. I growl in her ears and elsewhere, snarling my way over her body.

"Hey, aren't you gonna shoot yourself anymore? Go

on, shoot! Shoot, shoot, shoot, shoooooot . . .
Aaaaaaaaahhh . . ."

Later, when I thought it over, I realized what a stupid
phrase it was.

Now Dorothea is lying there, her golden body
stretched on the guanaco fur, beautiful and elegant like
a photograph in *Harper's Bazaar,* but more chic. Much
more chic, another class. I am unhappy and prostrated.
Dorothea looks at me.

"Who knows what Alvise sees in you? He adores you.
He really has a crush on you."

For a moment, I am perturbed.

"What kind of nonsense is that, baby? We're friends.
And what's more, we're both madly in love with you—
cruel beauty!"

After that imbecility, I throw myself on her, rolling
her under me, despite her protests.

But my ball-buster superego starts snickering in my
head.

"Dumb stud. You feel somewhat placated and less
unhappy than before. You stupidly act like a playboy
with that modest physique of yours. But Destiny, with
its tacky taste for bedroom farce, is about to smack you
back into squalid reality."

The *kvetch* is clairvoyant. In fact, as I am flirting with
Dorothea, I suddenly hear the sound of a car engine.
Something jumps in my mouth—it must be my heart.

"Oh, Christ! It's Alice! Hurry, get up, it's my wife."

Dorothea seems quite amused. I look like a madman
as I frantically wrap her back in her veils.

"Run! Out the back door, the servant's door . . . The kids . . . Hurry, goddammit!"

Dorothea allows herself to be dragged out the back way.

I feel a hammering in my chest.

Schmuck! Scumbag! I forgot that I had to go and pick up Alice and the kids at the airport! I run back into the apartment like a lunatic. As I check my appearance in the mirror, my ball-breaking conscience provokes me.

"*You* forgot, *bubeleh*, but guess who met her by chance in the airport and just happened to bring her home, instead of you?"

"Who? No, don't tell me, bastard!"

I run into the entrance hall and open the front door.

The horrible suspicion becomes a certainty. Alvise is helping Alice out of the car with her bags.

Of course! Wouldn't you just know it? Alvise just happened to be in the airport by sheer coincidence! Sheer coincidence . . . He saw her and took her home. Alice is in a fury, but Alvise is so kind and concerned that she controls her temper in front of him. And how she smiles and waves at him! She hates me and adores him, of course!

"Thanks a lot for picking us up. If it weren't for that angel, Alvise."

I stand there like an idiot. Fortunately, my embarrassment goes unobserved among the suitcases, hellos, kisses and the children's leaps and screams.

Destiny seems to get a kick out of fooling us poor mortals. Like a crazy interior decorator amusing himself by drawing curlicues, knots and labyrinths into the patterns of our lives. Because, lo and behold, as if Destiny had evoked her, in walks Betsy, our unfaithful, though overpaid maid.

I feel a chill. Shit, I hadn't thought about that. What if Betsy had arrived only fifteen minutes ago, and according to an inveterate habit of hers, had entered the kitchen with her keys, had poured me a glass of orange juice, had calmly and unsuspectingly come into my study, right in the middle of my superstud performance with Dorothea?

Something icy trickles down my back. It must be a drop of cold sweat.

I act as if nothing has happened. After all, everything has gone smoothly, they've even been picked up at the airport.

Alice is still thanking Alvise, who is taking his leave.

"Sorry, but I really must run now. 'Bye, Sam. See you soon. Good-bye, Alice."

As soon as he leaves, Alice sends the children off with Betsy and runs into my study.

She wants to know whether or not my identity crisis is over.

She is offended, of course, I know her well. Long ago, she would have whined for a week, but given my precarious emotional state, she controls herself.

"How are you feeling?"

"Lousy."

I glance at her and notice that she is truly worried about me. I feel guilty. After all, she has nothing to do with my sordid affairs.

I kiss her and pinch her cheek.

"No, I'm a little better. But you see? I forget everything."

Alice's attention is drawn to the pile of books and notes on my desk.

"Ah, you started working again."

Oh, hell! That drives me up the wall. She's already sticking her nose in.

"No, I'm not writing anything. I don't like being checked up on either. Mind your own business, and don't be such a *nudge*, Alice!"

I fly into a rage and throw her out. I hear her crying outside the door. I go back to my desk, feeling calmer. Yeah, I don't know what it is, but when I hear Alice crying, it brings me a peace of mind which puts me in a good mood. Go on and cry. Cry . . . Then, one of these nights, my orangutan will make it up to you, but just leave me alone, Wifey.

I suddenly hear a little sound. Chipper and Chucky sneak softly into my study. They're my biggest admirers. They usually take my side, and their mother—the "old witch"—as you've heard before, is the common enemy. I, the bastard, take advantage of everything Alice does to bring them up properly. The kids are my accomplices, I am their biggest pal, and together we feel that Alice is a chronic pain in the ass. I wink at them and slip them money under the counter.

They come into my study to see me. My little cubs give me a lot of satisfaction. Among their peers, I am a hero. Despite the fact that adults try to keep my books out of the hands of children, I know I sell like hotcakes among the youngsters.

Chucky comes toward me, talking like one of my characters.

"Hey, Calagan, the next time you stay at home alone and fool around with the blondes, gimme a whistle and I'll come running."

Somehow, it doesn't seem like he's joking. He goes over and sits in one of the desk drawers.

Chipper, on the other hand, is shimmying up my legs, holding something mysterious in her little hand.

"What do I have in my hand? Guess, Calagan!"

As I mentioned before, Calagan is a famous inspector who is often the protagonist of my novels.

"Don't bug me."

She is stubborn.

"Come on, guess what it is."

She climbs on top of me. I have to be tough with her.

"I don't know and I don't care. Come on, you pesky little kid, give old Calagan a kiss and out with you, because I have to work."

"If I were you, I'd be more curious. We want ten bucks to tell you what we know. Otherwise, you're screwed, Calagan."

Get a load of that!

"Ten bucks! Are you guys out of your skulls?! I don't give in to blackmailers!"

"You'd better pay, Calagan. Ten bucks or it's tough luck for you. Pay if you want to know!"

"I don't want to know, and I won't give you a cent. Dirty blackmailers."

Chucky keeps insisting.

"Hand over the ten. It'll be worth your while!"

The telephone rings. I answer it and try to free myself of the children at the same time.

"Never. Hello? Come on, gimme a kiss and let me work, you rascals. Hello?"

Alvise's voice is on the other end. He just got home. His voice is velvety.

"Is Alice still angry? I tried to calm her down."

I try to give my voice a suitable tone, but it isn't easy since Chipper is scrambling thoughtlessly over my legs with her pointed knees, crushing and tickling me; Chucky is pointing a loaded cap gun at me, which will make a terrible bang if fired.

"Oh, it isn't a big deal, Alvise. Alice is pretty good-natured. Thanks anyway."

Chipper continues with her threats and her whining voice which is starting to give me one hell of a pain in the ass.

"Hand over the ten bucks, Calagan. Ten bucks."

And Chucky adds:

"Give up, Calagan. It's better for you."

Now, they are really getting to me.

"Kids, you've really busted my—How is it you can't tell when a parent has important things to do? Sorry, Alvise."

I throw Chipper to the ground and grab the gun out of Chucky's hand. They start screaming and go on with their stupid blackmail game.

"So, you're not gonna give us the ten bucks?"

"Cut it out. Leave me in peace. If you don't get out

of here, I'm gonna give you both a big spanking. Out!"

I get back on the phone.

"Sorry, it's the kids."

Chipper is still waiting by the door with the mysterious object held tight in her hand. She is still threatening me. I chase her off with a wave of my hand. I turn back to the phone.

"Listen, thanks a lot for saving me at the airport today."

"Oh, stop it. It was nothing. What are you doing tonight? Maybe you want to stay home with Alice and the children, since they've just come back."

"Yeah, but I must confess that I really don't feel like it. I don't want to start up the old routine and go back to writing my monthly thrillers, that's all. I don't know. I may want to take a trip. I'd like to go and write somewhere else. Maybe a hot place, like Africa. It's probably just a stupid idea."

"Why not? Taking a trip . . ."

I can't listen to his words in peace because Alice now appears in the doorway. She stands in her slip, with her hand held out, as if offering something. A dramatic expression on her face. The funny thing is that her outstretched hand is completely empty. It makes me nervous.

I can't make any sense of it! What in hell could have gotten into that nerd now? She's standing in the doorway looking like Themis, the goddess of Justice, with that empty, outstretched hand. What a moron. What could have gone wrong this time? Her face is dead serious.

"Sorry, Alvise. I'll call you back later."

I hang up.

"Well? What is it?"

Alice looks like Ghengis Khan.

"You're asking me? You're the one who should be telling me what this is."

Alice continues holding out her empty hand.

I disengage myself from the desk. I am already beside myself.

"What the hell is this? Are you insane? I thought I was supposed to be the one with the nervous breakdown. What are you doing now? Playing copy cat?!"

Alice just stands there with that outstretched hand. Handing me nothing.

"Your daughter gave me this. She found it on the sofa, and there are many more of them. The whole guanaco fur is full of these revolting blond hairs! Do you think I'm stupid or something? So that's what your identity crisis and 'I'm not going to write anymore' and all those scenes of yours were about!"

I can now vaguely distinguish a few strands of blond hair in Alice's hand. Alice looks like Crazy Horse before he committed suicide.

I can see Chucky and Chipper snickering and watching me from the other end of the living room. Right, it's the first blackmail job of their little lives as criminals. That's why the two little monsters wanted the ten bucks. And without even warning me, they handed the bomb over to Alice, the brats. It's lucky we're friends, otherwise they might have even stabbed me in the back. Dammitall! Sure. They're Dorothea's hairs. So long and blond, I must have pulled out whole handfuls while the orangutan rutted away furiously.

Alice looks like a vengeful old Inca now.

"Well, what do you have to say for yourself? How shall we put it?"

I try to act pissed off.

"What do I know? I don't know what you're talking about. Go ask Betsy."

"Betsy!? Do I have to remind you that her hair is black, short and frizzy? Now the only thing left is for you to tell me that poor Betsy, with all her forty-eight years, is fooling around with some long-haired blond hippie, and that they come here and roll around on our couch! You filthy slob!"

"Alice! Not in front of the children!"

Alice is in a rage. All the anger she had kept under control in the last two weeks pours out, making her appear quite ferocious.

"Better that they know what kind of father they have, the poor little angels! A father who doesn't even have enough respect for his own home where his children live! Admit it! You brought your lover here! What is she, a hippie? A drug addict, or an ordinary whore? You pig!"

It's useless to try and stop her. This new explanation which she gives to my identity crisis is typical of a bourgeois moron. It makes her go on the rampage. She uses certain tones she inherited from her maternal grandmother that sound like cries in a Lebanese marketplace.

I feel like yelling: "After all, what do I know about it?"

She is already coming to a final, dramatic conclusion.

"No! Just don't say anything! I don't want to know anything! We'll call the lawyer! Thank God there's such a thing as divorce! Enough is enough! You and your scenes. I'm getting out of here and I'm taking the kids with me, you stinking creep! They're going to grow up in a sane and healthy place, a peaceful little town house."

"What did you say? A town house? Ah, so that's how it is. Now you're really flipping your lid! What town house? What are you babbling on about? Huh?"

"Well, you can hardly think that you ruin my life and get off scot-free. Oh, no, you'll pay for it. I want two hundred thousand dollars a year! You get about three hundred thousand, don't you? With all that shit you write?!"

See, the sweet companion of my life, the angel of my hearth? Nothing but insults and insane ravings!

"Two hundred thousand dollars!? A town house?! Poor darling's off her rocker. But what if I don't even feel like writing anymore?—put that in your pipe and smoke it."

"What *you* wanna do, *I* don't even wanna know about! Go and roll around with your blond bitches wherever you feel like it! You're going to give me that two hundred thousand dollars, or else I'll report you to the IRS."

With this terrible threat, Alice leaves my study, slamming the door against my nose. All of a sudden, I feel a violent cramp. Sure, it's the ulcer! It's eating my stomach! Alice, the nut, who today, for the first time, I realize is absolutely insane, is denouncing me to the tax collector. The mother of my children, the companion of my life, the woman who took the protective place of my poor mamma!

The anger inside me rises. I open the door and bellow like a maniac.

"What do you mean? Just whom are you reporting?!"

Alice turns on me like a hyena. Betsy and the children come running in order not to miss the show.

"I'm reporting *you!* You and all the messes you made to avoid paying taxes, and the money in Switzerland, and all the rest! You pig!"

She's lost her head all right. She's talking about our taxes in front of the help!

"Alice! Betsy's here!"

"Great! So Betsy, the boss says that you are the lover of some blond, long-haired hippie, and that you come here and fool around with him!"

Betsy jumps up in a fury. She too is against me.

"What? I'm a respectable woman. Go tell that dirt to the marines! And I have no boss!"

The children laugh and get two slaps. Consequently, the children cry. Betsy yells. So does Alice.

It's all over. My world and my home are destroyed, and I don't even have a corner left where I can find some peace. Whose fault is it all? Yes, it's his. That Alvise who smiles, unaware of what he has done. I hate him. I want his head, and I'll have it too!

I leave the house, slamming the door.

Here I am, sitting like an idiot between my guardian devils. Yes. I am at their house. Alvise and Dorothea are by my side. They heard about my family argument, but naturally do not know how it began.

Affectionately, they welcome me, give me a drink, and then Alvise comes out with an amazing question.

"If you're seriously thinking about traveling—you mentioned Africa—what do you think of the Middle East?"

"The Middle East? I hadn't considered it in the least. Oh, what an ass! I'm talking in rhyme. Anyway, sorry, what do you mean?"

Damn him. He always makes me feel unprepared or . . . I don't know . . . awkward, dumb. But he, he has the feline poise of a hoopoe. And don't tell me that the hoopoe bird is not feline! I know that! And I don't give a damn! The hoopoe could very well have some feline grace. On the other hand, is Alvise a feline? No, he's only a regular, perfect guy, a genius, saint and Santa Claus, fitting somewhere in stature between Moses and Solomon.

For a moment, many strange thoughts and doubts flutter like bats through my head. Then, Alvise's voice, like a purifying breeze, sweeps everything away.

"I'm leaving tomorrow for Jerusalem. Why don't you come along? Alice already had her vacation. She'll understand. A nice trip to the holy land of our ancient roots?"

"With you? To Jerusalem?"

"First I said no, but then I changed my mind and accepted. It's for a group of friends in Amnesty International. We'll be passing through Tel Aviv. Don't you feel like seeing the Middle East? I'd be happy to show you Israel: flowers in the desert, and death as a roommate. It's educational. You need to get out of New York and take a look around the world. Maybe we'll go to Iran after that. Or even Afghanistan."

I am stunned.

"Go away? Take a trip together? You mean it?"

"Certainly. In those parts of the world where the great cycles of humanity from time to time intertwine and explode."

I close my eyes tightly.

I'm not listening to him anymore. A series of titles runs through my head: *Mystery in the Kibbutz; Is There a Cadaver Cemented in the Wailing Wall?; Death on a Superjet.* While Alvise continues talking, I am busy planning what I should pack. The essentials kit for the traveling perpetrator of the next perfect crime. I want the very best in thriller-type planning and inventions for committing that crime.

Yes! It's something to do! Destiny is a bus you have to catch on the run.

Yes! I hop on Destiny's bus. But I have to do things well, in the best way, with class. Put yourselves in my shoes. A wizard of thrillers, mystery and suspense who wants to carry out the perfect crime can't afford to screw it up. He has to be a professional.

I am in a telephone booth on the street. It's nighttime.

The cold glare of the streetlights give me the impression I am acting out a scene in a film.

I like the idea of giving Alice a terrible fright. It has been twenty-four hours since I left without saying a word to her. Forget the threats about the lawyer; I imagine she's desperate.

By the icy light of a neon sign, I dial my home number. Alice answers.

"Hello?"

"Alice, would you do me the favor of telling Betsy to pack two suitcases full of my summer clothes? I'll stop by and pick them up in a half-hour, thank you."

I hang up.

She doesn't know where I am. I am sure that she's having a hysterical fit and wetting her pants in fear.

This way, the cretin will learn to joke about fiscal blackmail.

Alice is waiting behind the door with two packed suitcases. Her eyes are puffy, and the hallway light reveals the merry little sparkle of a teardrop in her lashes.

I must say I feel sorry for her as she stands there, miserable, ailing, with her swollen eyes, her unkempt hair, her trembling lips. Poor Alice, she's just an innocent victim in the whole mess.

"Where are you going?"

"The Middle East. Israel, I don't know."

I don't have the courage to go on because she throws herself into my arms, sobbing. That's the way she's always tricked me. She isn't the harpy or the blackmailer of yesterday. She is only a poor woman in love, dammit. I love her too. She pulls me back inside the house.

See what tricks life can play on you? For ten minutes, I'd even forgotten about Alvise. Aside from the blondes and all the rest, my Alice and I march along very well together. We are one of those couples who, thank God, make up their fights in bed. Got it?

* * *

In fact, we are down at the foot of the bed when I hear Alvise honking outside.

I get up.

Alice had convinced herself that the storm was over because she had forgiven me. She lies there like an idiot as she watches me get dressed.

"Where are you going?"

"I told you, dear, to Israel."

Alice sits up.

"What do you mean? You're going away? Just like that?"

"Yes. So long, darling. Kiss the children for me."

And I walk out of the room just like one of my heroes, leaving Alice behind on the big bed, stunned by our lovemaking and my departure. I go!

Alvise is below. Fate is offering me the chance of a great, liberating adventure. The wind is favorable—I feel it!

The Middle East will be the turning point for my future.

A throng of reporters are waiting at the airport. They crowd around Alvise and pepper him with questions.

"Mr. Ottolenghi Portaleoni, are you for or against Qaddafi's policies? Will this be one of the topics covered in the Tel Aviv talks? Which regime are you more in favor of—the Islam of Khomeini, or that of Arafat? Are you bringing the White House's opinion to the assembly on pan-Arabism? Is it true that the Ayatollah cuts off thieves' hands and cuts out perjurers' tongues? Someone said that where the Koran rules, there's no need for a constitution. How do you feel about that?"

It is the first time that none of the reporters recognize me. My stomach is being eaten away by a raging acid. It's the ulcer. Any doubts I might have had about the urgency of resolving the Alvise "affair" now vanish like fog in the sun. I feel neglected and unhappy.

We have already reached the plane's door. The reporters are still firing away. We wave at Dorothea, who has come to see us off.

The plane takes off, ascends and makes a wide turn in the sky. The bay beneath us shimmers in the hot morning sun. Well . . . Yeah. Look who's here. In New York, a lot of time goes by before seeing one another again, isn't that true, Madam? Farewell, Statue of Liberty. We rise higher in the sky as we move away from the thrusting skyscrapers of old Manhattan. The Statue of Liberty grows smaller and smaller, until it's nothing but a speck on the bay. I remember then, when I was returning to America with Alvise after the tragedy in the camps. I remember when I saw you with your torch, beautiful lady. I was a child. Damn! For me, it was almost like seeing my mother again. I'm filled with a terrible nostalgia for those times.

Yeah, it's nostalgia, all right. Ayayayay. It's hard remembering those good old "bad times," living in the bad new "good times."

Do I sound drunk? Yes, I'm going overboard. I'm talking incoherently. But thinking back on it, to the war in 1940, I mean . . .

It was a great period for the U.S. The roles in the comedy were clear: The bad guys were the German

Nazis and the Italian Fascists, along with the treacherous, yellow Japs.

We were the good guys. We Americans stood arm in arm with the European allies, which then included the Russians.

We were the so-called "crème de la crème."

Yeah, we were the heroes all right.

Our boys were big, loyal, tall, blond, healthy, kind and handsome. Armies of Gary Coopers beneath the stars and stripes.

A delightful march accompanied by Fred Astaire's tapping feet. Yes, we sometimes bombed civil populations, but *à la guerre comme à la guerre*.

Those years were still far from Hiroshima. Vietnam and all the subsequent confusion lay even further away. Allende, the Shah of Iran, the Bay of Pigs, the two Kennedy deaths, Pol Pot, the genocide and the raising of stakes in Afghanistan, Khomeini and the hostages . . .

We were still living in a full-fledged fairy tale.

America, it's the first time that I've left you since then. And a vague sense of fear grips my stomach. You can say whatever you want, but within your arms, I feel secure. Dear lady. While far from your torch, there are more and more risks. I am leaving, but don't worry, your Sammy, that is, little Salome, will come back. Victorious. I hope so. Oh . . . I think of Dorothea. She's there affectionately waving good-bye to me like a friend. But, goddammitall! She comes to me to get laid, and then looks at Alvise with those lovesick eyes, splendid—Vivian Leigh-*Waterloo Bridge*! Why does she look at him like that? It's enough to make me bang my head against the wall! It's really true. It takes a special mind to understand some women.

A random flyer who happened to be flying over that part of the world known as the Middle East, and who happened to cast a casual, bird's-eye glance at the area, couldn't help but notice a lively series of bright, bursting dots followed by white and black balloons of smoke.

If that random and careless flyer were to innocently ask his neighbor for an explanation, he would find out that the bright spots and balloons are not Arabian bazaars, patron saint festivities or celebrations and tributes to the Prophet, but rather hot spots in the Middle-Eastern fireplace.

That is: raids, fires, bombs, machine-gunnings, military actions, battles, regular war, urban guerrilla warfare, safari guerrilla warfare, Superpower armies and shepherd guerrillas; Afghanistan, Pakistan, Turkey, Arabia, Iran, Libya . . . It seems the more you had, the more you used.

Terrorist attempts, commando actions, fratricidal battles, hand-to-hand combat, punitive expeditions, army occupations, revolutions, territorial claims, chain reactions of vendettas, Molotov cocktails, explosions and Black Septembers.

Now, when the flyer sitting next to you happens to be Alvise—that is, a political super-expert, leader of Amnesty International—the unfortunate and careless flyer, who in this case is me, must submit to a thorough and accurate historical-socio-political lesson on the Middle

East, with an in-depth description of its coastal Mediterranean civilizations—Arab and Turkish, the great Islam,
Mohammed and Marx, ideologies, religions, beliefs,
structures, myths, economy, ecology. I look at him, my
eyes bulging. I listen. Alvise's perfection generates in me
complete envy.

How in the hell does he know all this stuff? I feel like
shit, with my stomach contracting from an ulcer attack.
I keep repeating the same refrain to myself: "Take it
easy, Sammy, old buddy. Take it easy.

"Let him be. It's his swan song. You've got six
schemes for a perfect crime in your attaché case. It's just
a matter of time. Hold out a bit longer. Soon this su-
perbeing's beautiful head will be falling at your feet."

As I ponder over my six perfect crimes, super-Alvise
is finally coming to the end of his history lesson.

"Yes, we did buy those pieces of land from the own-
ers. But undeniably, that land was the home of many
Arabs who had to not only change who ruled them but
also the way they lived. And even worse, when protests
ended badly, the Arabs chose to emigrate, and landed in
the ghettos and refugee camps of the neighboring Arab
countries. It's the sort of thing that ought to make people
think."

"About what?"

All the passengers are listening, fascinated.

"About the fact that human nature, even at its best,
may have a black root which seeks to reproduce the evil
it receives, as if to free itself. I mean that the people of
Israel, who have been oppressed and mistreated for thou-

sands of years, should have a different relationship with the minorities who risk being oppressed and mistreated like they were. And so, the people of Israel live in the danger that the arms which had originally been meant for defense, and which suddenly took on a different role after the victory, could become arms for offense and conquest."

Alvise is now giving his press conference over Israeli television.

It's on the same subject he spoke about on the plane: He speaks as the ancient prophets and brilliant lawyers must have once done. Certainly, seeing him on television, I have to admit that he is handsome and fascinating.

"If Israel's arms are solely for offense and conquest, and this is the spirit that prevails, then it is a dark stain that soils the pure conscience of our ancient land. Yes, we made the desert bloom. Yes, we set an example of harmony between man and nature with our communal work, and that is something that will go down in history, the history of those men who seek new structures for a more just society. Yes, we created a new and different community. I have the greatest regard for this exceptional work, even though I share Heinroth's fears when he said: 'After the wingflapping of the Argus pheasant, the working rhythm of humanity is the stupidest product of interspecific selection.' But we'll leave it to the sociologist to declare that hate and love are neither good nor bad, just as the thyroid is neither good nor bad in itself. I believe in love. That is why I am sure that the Scriptures of the Ancient Fathers must guide us toward the light of a better future. Let the deepest meaning of the spirituality of our people conquer the darkness that threatens to throw our civilization into a new Middle Ages. Peace, brothers."

The Israeli television transmits Alvise's image and his words in all the squares, streets, bars and houses of Tel Aviv.

People of all kinds sit glued to their television sets, listening to Alvise speak. His are obviously the words of a wise man and leader.

Alvise's speech is also being transmitted on the television set in Room 13 in the Hotel Tel Aviv.

In front of the television, there is a table. I am working behind that table. I am busy withdrawing several drops of curare from a little bottle with an eyedropper. I squeeze them into the ice-cube containers and put the containers in the freezer, where they solidify in a few minutes. I check my first set of ice cubes, and note that there are no visible traces of the curare. Excellent. Naturally, it's a perfect plan. Curare in ice cubes, to drink with a super-iced vodka, a great refresher from the intense heat. It ought to produce the same symptoms as congestion. The curare is laced with a slow-working emetic that will induce vomiting and anal expulsion of the poison and its traces, prior to cardiac arrest. Everything is taken care of up to the smallest details. I am in the final phase. But Alvise is still talking on the television and it's almost impossible to resist the lure of his words.

Sure, no one in Israel was interested in letting some pain-in-the-ass prophet pull skeletons out of the closet that risked reopening all the old wounds.

The reporters have obviously been sent to the press conference to cut his throat.

They gun him down with embarrassing questions and attack him like piranhas.

Alvise answers every question and is now concluding with a personal message. That speech. Those words. The alluring, enchanting voice is irresistible. Alvise is like a snake-charmer, seducing and hypnotizing the entire collective ego. He isn't only charming the whole city, the whole community, all of Israel—clear to the burning frontiers, the desert kibbutzim and those reporters with crocodile hearts and boa-constrictor stomachs, but unfortunately, he's also charming me.

I am listening to him with tears in my eyes.

I distractedly throw one of the ice cubes into my glass of Coca-Cola. With my eyes still stuck to the screen, hypnotized by a close-up of Alvise's face, I raise the glass to my lips. I sniffle with emotion and take a sip. The contact with the cold drink is enough to rouse me immediately, and I am stricken with terror.

I spit out the liquid. I jump up, I glance back at the television screen with hatred. Alvise is still uttering his pearls of wisdom. I run to the bathroom. I spit frantically and rinse my mouth out with water.

The reflection in the mirror sneers at me. That fucking superego.

"Asshole! The master of thrillers!"

I whirl around like a madman.

I glare at the mirror and then collapse to the ground in a fit of convulsions.

Perfect. The same symptoms as congestion. Vomiting and anal rejection, but not because of the curare. I swallowed such a small amount. My feeling ill is caused by my fear and sudden hysteria.

And this is how Alvise will find me.

Jerusalem is one of those fatal places where human tensions build up, ferment and finally explode.

If you think about it in perspective, it's quite frightening. Canaan, the Jebusites, Saul, King David, Solomon, and right on down to Rome, Christ and the Crusades.

Luckily, I have a healthy lack of culture. Otherwise, I would be terrified to think about it all.

Perhaps the most striking fact in the city's history was the Judaic-Christian encounter.

An ancient accredited boxing ring for the two religions, if I make myself clear, Jerusalem is one of those places that dozes for centuries in the sun, chewing on seeds and fingering prayer beads with closed eyes, amid the buzzing of flies. But woe to those who trust it. Because one day—zap!—when you least expect it, these places become the protagonists of history again.

Fatal places! The most sacred part of the sacred city is a privileged area of the "territorial, historical, cultural, religious Jerusalem"—as they say in cultured newspapers—the famous Wailing Wall.

The Wall faces on a beautiful square—an imposing and ancient space, with a human dimension. The kind of space modern architects are always looking for but no longer find. The measure of man—the measure of faith. Nothing to do with an analyst's couch! The Wailing Wall is really something!

Yeah, psychoanalysis should study these parts, where ancient religions operate.

Many believers are praying in intense concentration along the great, solemn Wailing Wall.

It is a heavy, sultry day. The blue skies weigh heavily upon us, more than if the day had been cloudy and gray.

Everything is whitish, bleached by centuries of sun. The color of the desert sand, a sea of powder which stretches far beyond the ancient Wall, for hundreds of miles into space and time.

Even the flies barely fly because of the heavy air that burdens their wings.

The whispering of many voices in the air sounds like the droning of a beehive.

Jews of every age and every walk of life rock themselves rhythmically to the music of the murmured prayers. They pour out their grief to God through the Wall.

Yes, I am here too.

I also *daven,* and whisper my desperate thoughts.

Perhaps it's a prayer.

"I'm a *schmuck*, an idiot. I made an ass out of myself! Oh, Lord, why did you let *him* of all people find me? The super-perfect Alvise. Why did you let him take me in his arms, like a mother, to the hospital? Now he's got the impression again that he's saved my life.

"Oh, Lord, be generous. Grant the prayers of your servant Sammy. Send for your servant Alvise, what'll it cost you? Don't the best always die first? We're even overpopulated. The ecologists swear that there are too many of us in the world. Do it too for the sake of the ecological balance."

Next to me stands a miserable little man in rags, praying intensely. His rumbling prayer is getting on my nerves.

"Oh, Lord, my family is hungry. I beg you. If only I could have a little money so I could feed them. I beg you, Lord. Just a little money."

Just like one of those stupid Yiddish tales about Leib Jacob, the rich fur merchant, and Janow, the poor man, in the village of Radoszyce.

I watch him with annoyance. Then I look up at the sky. The miserable little fellow is stubborn all right.

"I beg you, Lord. Just some money to feed them."

He is driving me up the wall. I raise my eyes to the sky. The Lord is a very busy lord. Why should this fellow distract him with a dumb thing like that? He is taking time away from me.

I decide to behave like Jacob, the rich fur merchant. I pull on his sleeve. The wretched man turns around and faces me with two watery eyes.

"Here."

I quickly reach into my pocket and pull out ten dollars.

I put the money in his hand. I don't want him distracting the Lord with that crap. I have serious troubles.

"There, take it and go away, please."

The wretched man can't believe his eyes. He tries to kiss my hand.

"Thank you, thank you, sir."

I push the man away, and he walks off happily. Finally alone, I continue my prayer.

"Sorry. Don't let yourself get sidetracked, Lord. What was I saying? Oh, what'll it cost you, Lord? After all, if a god doesn't grant a favor once in a while, he loses some authority. And then you can't be too surprised about the decrease in vocations and the growing materialism. In fact, we could make some kind of pact. I mean, I could also lend you a hand some time, like what if I had Mike Bullit converted to your faith? Do you realize the commercial potential? Do you know how many copies are sold in the United States alone? Think it over, Lord. It's a real bargain for you—unless, of course, you happen to be on Alvise's side. That's all I need—you on the side of the perfect one. Two super-perfects! That wouldn't be very respectable, God, don't you agree? You've got to stay with the weak and needy. So you have no choice. You have to be on my side. After all, what am I asking for? Only Alvise's head."

My whispered prayer is suddenly interrupted by two hands grabbing hold of my shoulders. I jump as if it were the police grabbing me.

"Who is it?"

"Who is it?"

"No. Who is it? I asked first."

"Brother."

Incredible! Coincidence! *Coup de théâtre!* A trick of destiny!

It's old Solomon from our childhood travels. He's a prophetic apparition.

For a moment, I do not recognize him. He stands, wrapped in long, ancient religious robes, with a thick beard, and white hair that falls over his shoulders in ringlets. He wears a *yarmulka* on his head.

"Oh, God! It's you, Solomon!"

"You recognized me, brother."

"Yes, I recognized you, but how did you manage to recognize me? I was only a little boy back then."

"I'm a prophet."

"Of course. Sure. Maybe you really are a prophet, you haven't changed a bit."

The wretched man to whom I'd given the ten dollars sees us and approaches.

There is something different about him.

He goes up to Solomon.

"Forgive me, *Nebturay Kartah*. I didn't know he was a protégé of yours. I'll give him back his ten dollars."

Solomon smiles through his thick beard and winks at me as he did many years ago.

"My brother knows the ways of the world."

Then he turns to me with the complicity of an old Catholic alms robber.

"You know, life is rough. You can get by in places of worship, though. He stands by the people who look rich. The tale about Master Jacob of the village of Radoszyce inspired him. It's better than begging in the name of the Lord, right? You can keep your ten dollars, David. You earned them."

The man walks off. Solomon turns to look at me with his luminous eyes.

"And Alvise. The wise man has come back to talk to his people. Is he here with you?"

"Yes. No. Well, he left this morning for the border with an international commission. They're going to visit a refugee camp. He'll be back tomorrow."

"It's beautiful meeting you here, in prayer. You looked so absorbed and devoted. What were you asking the Lord?"

"Huh? Oh, nothing. Silly stuff."

A loud roar rips through the air.

A fleet of jet bombers rumbles over our heads. Solomon points to them, his eyes brimming with tears.

"God. Oh, God. See what the law is? Vengeance! An eye for an eye. They're going off to bomb the Syrian border."

Something in his words strikes me. I don't understand exactly what he said. The Syrian border? Exactly where Alvise went? My hair stands on end. I feign indifference.

"They're going to the Syrian border? Where the camps are? I mean, where Alvise is?"

"Death summons death. Blood summons blood. I'm going to pray."

I am excited. They are going to bomb the place where Alvise has gone. Well, it is a benevolent sign from heaven. I tug on Solomon's robe.

"Oh, pray for me too. It's a bad time. I need help."

"He, the Blessed One whose name cannot be uttered in vain, will help you if you pray."

"He will?"

I watch the jets disappear over the horizon.

Yes, it is possible. Perhaps the blessed unmentionable has finally decided to lend me a hand.

* * *

People always talk about the beauty of the desert. All right, there are beautiful colors—an entire range of shades of beige, from pale butter to lightning-burned black. It is also famous for its shimmering mirages.

The air is dry. The bleached earth has been dehydrated for centuries. It looks as bad as it possibly could. The terrible African sun is hidden, sulking in the haze. We are traveling for miles and miles past dust and holes, our backs broken, our mouths tasting sand instead of saliva.

After many hours, we finally come to a halt.

It is an Arab military blockade. Rifles are leveled at us. We show them our pass. "Authorized Commission of the International Red Cross." It isn't pleasant identifying yourself with those black holes pointing at the space between your eyes.

Excluding my famous experiences during childhood, it is the first time real loaded guns were pointed at me. The finger of a mysterious Arab, his dark face swathed in cloth, on the trigger. He could even be a vicious, sadistic, racist assassin, for all I know. Damn! I feel the degrading sensation of an icy hand squeezing my intestines. I feel a terrible need to go to the bathroom.

It may be a basic need, but believe me, it isn't easy to ask permission to gratify it when you have guns pointing at you in the middle of the desert.

In fact, it is so difficult, that I am forced to give up the idea and repress it. Repression is an ugly thing, as we all know.

Our documents are finally returned. With a crisp salute, the jeep proceeds on its way.

My face is pale beneath the Arab headdress that I wear to protect me from the sand.

Well, well. It seems that "He whose name cannot be uttered" has decided to collaborate. Yes. Several bombs have hit an area including the very refugee camp where the Amnesty International commission was visiting. In other words, Alvise!!!!

Therefore, being a close friend of his, I've been asked to be present on the painful occasion, to identify the corpse of Professor Ottolenghi Portaleoni. I feel rather excited.

The bombed Palestinian camp is reduced to a heap of shacks in pitiful condition. We stand in front of the entrance and I am taken aback by the harsh reality. The ground is simply devastated.

Death, blood, ripped mattresses, pieces of chairs, distorted camp kitchens, bloodied rags, a slipper, desperate eyes and emaciated faces surround us.

We put masks over our mouths like they taught us as a hygiene precaution. The road in this hell of pain is paved with death, and God knows how many good intentions. It's true. I really have to fight off that old feeling of anguish that returns from childhood and raises a lump in my throat.

I am as excited as a young bride on her wedding night, as I think of my encounter with Alvise's remains. What a poor naïve idiot I am. How could I predict that a serious "being," hardly inclined to joking around, like "He whose name must not be mentioned in vain," would play such a nasty trick on me, Sam Silverman! A trick, yes. A scurvy trick. I wander through a sea of death. The stench of dismembered bodies is nauseating. Endless horror. I feel sick. And Alvise is nowhere to be seen.

By the time the cordon of Arabs lets the commission leave, my face is ashen.

The others are shaken as well. The fedayeen's eyes are full of hatred.

My precocious training in atrocities, which I owe to the prize firm of Hitler & Himmler, helps very little. Dammitall, the others manage to get by with only pale faces. But not me. Perhaps I am still under the effect of the emetic in the curare. My head begins to reel and a huge hand seems to be yanking my stomach out through my mouth. Nothing worse than throwing up on an empty stomach. I'm very sick. I feel as if I have to hold my stomach back with my teeth. Vomiting is such a horror. You're sick, you're disgusting, worse than when you shit, and it's the peak of humiliation.

I glance up at the sky. "The Ineffable He whose name cannot be uttered" must have had himself a good laugh. Alvise? Well, he isn't among the corpses, but try to guess where he is.

Where could that exquisite, luminous wonder of wonders be? Exactly where Gary Cooper would have been placed by a mediocre screenwriter in a *schmaltzy* Hollywood film of the thirties.

In the camp hospital! And what can Alvise be doing there? He is operating! Under trying conditions. Yes, he is struggling to save the bomb victims from the jaws of Death!

The commission is at the entrance of the tent, watching in awe. And green-faced, I stand in front of the others with my eyes wide open.

Alvise is busy operating on a woman.

A little Arab nurse is helping him, with admiration in her eyes.

The commission is disturbing him. Alvise glances at them angrily and nods to the nurse to send them away.

Of course! The maestro is struggling against Death. How dare we trouble him? The nurse sends the intruders away immediately.

I manage to stay behind in the tent where Alvise is concentrating on his surgery. Yes. It's useless to go into details, but during his voluntary service in the leper clinic, Alvise obtained a degree in general medicine, with specialization in cardiology, neurology, ear, nose and throat, and general surgery. Naturally, he is a superb doctor.

A violinist's hand, an eagle's eye and the cold passion of a benevolent genius in his face. Just watching him operate makes my ulcer throb in sharp, icy spasms. Then something grabs my attention.

My bulging eyes glance at the table that holds the surgical instruments. The row of sharp-bladed scalpels sparkles invitingly.

Sure, we are surrounded by hate-filled fedayeen. How many crimes take place in the Middle East at the hands of mysterious guerrillas after a bombardment? Of course. It is an opportunity. A great opportunity. Hit and run. Then, freedom.

Silently, I grab one of the scalpels. I am behind Alvise's back.

I am resolved to go through with my homicidal plans.

The act isn't going to be easy for me. I am a theorist. I am totally lacking in practical experience. In reality, violence makes me feel queasy. The sight of blood has a terrible effect on me. Nevertheless, I have to pluck up courage and free myself forever of my incubus.

Unfortunately, I happen to glance down on what Alvise is working on with so much ability, intensity and concentration. My God! There is a terrible gash in the abdomen, with all the guts sticking out. I start getting sick to my stomach again. I try to get a hold of myself. I summon up all my strength in order to make my big move. With my face screwed up in a grimace, I raise the tightly clenched scalpel.

Without turning around, Alvise reaches his hand out and takes the scalpel out of my hand.

"Thanks, I knew I could count on you. Scalpel number five. Prepare the thread for resection."

I obey like a robot. Nothing has changed, and I become involved in my new role as surgeon's assistant.

The little nurse comes back in and busies herself with basins and hot water. Alvise is the supreme authority, and the tension in the tent is palpable.

"Careful. Check the anesthesia and the pressure. Hurry, Fatima, the pressure is dropping. We need a transfusion. It's urgent."

"But we've finished the plasma."

"I'm sorry. It's a matter of life and death. We need blood. Take it from him."

Fatima quickly grabs hold of my arm. I want to protest, but I lose my voice. I can't refuse. The nurse is working on me rapidly.

"He whose name cannot be uttered" must have had himself some more laughs. I, Sam Silverman, who'd let the world come to an end to avoid having an injection. And here I am, hopelessly trapped in that tent, with some sort of dagger stuck in my forearm. I give my blood for the transfusion while standing and assisting in the operation. I think I have reached the limit.

But I find out it is only the beginning. Alvise goes on operating for three days and three nights, without sleeping, naturally. And me with him. Together, we saved the lives of thirty-five wounded. Only two died in surgery. I certainly would have been the third if at the last minute an attack of conscience hadn't softened the cruel fate that had been reserved for me by the "Blessed Ineffable, Unpronounceable He whose name cannot be uttered."

Luckily, I'm not the only one who thinks Alvise is a pain in the ass.

The fedayeen regard him with great suspicion because he is Jewish, and the Israelis shudder in the knowledge that he is loose in that camp and may meet up with Arafat at any moment.

There are also certain contacts he has with Iran that haven't escaped Egypt's notice. Alvise Ottolenghi Portaleoni, aka Isaac Smith, is a potential floating mine for a great many people.

Me included. I can't trigger off that damn mine. They finally load us on an airplane, and we get out of that place.

They "kindly" send us away, and just in time, because I'm about to cash in my chips. Damn!

* * *

In a first-class seat, I am a sort of weak, green skeleton, swathed in blankets.

Alvise, next to me, is taking loving care of me. He puts a straw in my mouth and has me suck up some gray muck from a glass.

A stewardess, madly in love with Alvise, is helping him. He is extraordinary, naturally.

"Come on, Sammy, be good. You must drink this beef broth."

"I don't want to. It's disgusting. I think I'm gonna vomit."

"Vomit and I'll make you drink more. Come on. Stop fooling around!"

Alvise practically forces the straw into my mouth. I begin to suck up the stuff, disgusted.

"You've got to get back your supply of red corpuscles. You've given blood ten times in the last three days."

The stewardess looks at Alvise dreamily.

"Really?"

"My poet friend has saved many lives with his blood."

He seems very proud of me.

"It was a beautiful gesture, Sammy."

"Yeah, but I was hardly dying to do it."

It's very difficult for me to talk with that damned straw in my mouth.

"You took advantage of my weakness. You're worse than a vampire. Nosferatu."

Alvise smiles.

"He's funny too. You're really unusual, Sammy! Gee, I wish you had been in Israel back then, during the early kibbutzim struggle to revive the land. To bring water back into the desert. To conjure fruit trees or spikes of wheat from the barren sand. For everyone, altogether."

I feel like barfing. I try to take that straw out of my mouth.

"I don't want anymore, I'm gonna puke."

Alvise is resolute. He holds my nose.

"Hold it back. Swallow. You need blood."

I courageously try to free myself. Alvise's strong hand holds me back and forces me to suck up the rest of the beef broth.

"Yes, things have changed. But fertile seeds and hard work can triumph over the desert. Ah, good. You've finished. Where's the baby food?"

The stewardess holds out a bottle.

"No, not that stuff! That's disgusting. It looks like dog food."

"You didn't make such a fuss about food when you were little. Remember?"

"What's that got to do with now? We were at Treblinka. Why are you dragging out those stories? I don't want this *dreck*!"

"Stop misbehaving. You've got to get better. We have to go to the Vatican to see Cardinal Ruggeri-Castelnuovo. Since he's a prince of the Catholic Church, he's in competition with us Jews. I don't intend for us to make a bad impression. So, eat! Oh, look! There's the kingdom of Satan."

The plane is completing its wide, solemn turn over the famous panorama of domes and hills. It is Rome.

I pull myself up, weak but curious.

"What do you mean, Satan? In Rome?"

"Satan is the patron of Rome."

"What lengths people go to beat a competitor."

"I wasn't the one who said it. It's from the Cabbala."

"That's just it! Come on. I'd like to know what the Pope has to say about that. Satan! The Ancient Fathers really got rough at times."

Anyway, long live Satan, or anyone else for that matter! I couldn't take that Middle Eastern volcano anymore. I'd really had it! On the other side of the fence were Mohammed, Allah and his prophets, the Koran and all those nice rules which permit them to cut off hands, ears and heads with complete tranquillity and the blessings of the Prophet.

The Catholic Church is quite another thing. Of course, she didn't fool around either, with the Inquisition, burnings at the stake and tearing out fingernails. Anyway, should a war break out, it is obviously better to be on Mohammed's or Russia's side. At least you'd be able to surrender to the dear old U.S., who'd only stick you in some camp with an ample supply of beer, Coca-Cola and McDonald's hamburgers. And then play gin rummy waiting for the end of the war. But if you were a prisoner on the *other* side . . . Well, there's an entire literature on the subject. At best they'd send you to Siberia, or respectfully speaking, screw you royally! And that's not excluding the possibility that they might even screw you royally *in* Siberia!

As I was saying—Long Live Satan, and a peaceful Roman vacation.

* * *

I am fascinated by all these baroque clouds that are certainly concealing fluttering angels playing silver trumpets. I look around me—terracotta roofs, people eating in sidewalk cafés, curves in the golden river, and curves of the domes resembling big bottoms and big tits, and phallic obelisks. There are piazzas, palazzi, parks and parking lots, traffic jams, very elegant shops, sphinxes, palms, marble stairways, and fluttering whirls of marmoreal draperies. I suspect that this famous city, like all old whores, will never let you down.

It is beautiful, old and totally unsuited for traffic. Our taxi is creeping along at a snail's pace. A thousand devils in the form of an ulcer are tearing at my stomach. My attaché case is my only comfort. I hold it tightly by my side and stroke it lovingly. It's very very very very chic. Better than James Bond's bag of tricks. Only four of the six schemes remain for a perfect crime that leaves no traces. I eliminated the other one that dealt with poison after my experience with the curare. Four left! They're the fruits of an accurate study of the methods elaborated by the superspecialized minds of the world's major crime theorists since the year 1780, at least judging from the number of copies sold. I just hope that Rome will give me a lucky break.

Naturally, some friend of Alvise's has lent him his penthouse apartment in an aristocratic seventeenth-century palazzo. It is a place you could gloat over.

The sumptuous apartment is scented with candles. Full of soft lights and splendid antique furniture that is almost hidden in the shadows. Distinguished ancestors look down from the walls with piercing, ironic eyes. A faint light filters through the stained-glass windows.

Perfection. Just what I needed for the execution of my most difficult scheme. Plan number four: "Accident in the Home." It calls for one of those unfortunate deaths that go down among the statistics of daily genocide that occur in apartments equipped with electrical appliances, in the big cities. This particular scheme is inspired by an old classic written by a little-known Scottish mystery writer, Euterpe Sherwood, a friend of Agatha Christie's. The title of the story is "Aunt Gertrude's Visit." The idea is simple, yet brilliant. All it requires is a suitable setting.

I find the perfect setting behind a massive old oak door, at the far end of the hall, in the back of the apartment.

Yes, it's nothing more than a bathroom, which is covered in antique tiles. There is an impressive bathtub with lion's feet made of enameled iron, which was common at the beginning of the century.

I don't sleep all night, and as soon as dawn begins to transform the dark, star-studded cloak of the sky into a pearly pink glow, I get up and tiptoe into the bathroom.

I see myself in the mirror with my electrician's do-it-yourself kit from *Popular Mechanics*.

I look at myself for a moment, like the wicked queen in *Snow White*.

" 'Mirror, mirror on the wall, who's the fairest of them all?' "

I know it will answer, "Alvise, stupid!"

I look away to avoid hearing the reply.

In this adventure, my critical superego is becoming even more of a ball-breaker than that ball-breaking Alvise.

I get down to work immediately. The concept of the operation is fairly simple. When Alvise goes into the bathroom in an hour's time . . . Phhhhhtttttt!!!!

I don't want to go into all the details now. I mean, it is so simple it almost seems stupid. All I have to do is connect an exposed wire to the chain on the plug in the bathtub. Then, after the event? I'd only have to remove the traces and throw an electric hairdryer into the bathwater, so that . . . Elementary, my dear Watson.

The hope of a successful outcome gives wings to my feet, or rather, to my hands.

Watch out, Sammy. Watch out. Be careful. You can't fool around with water and electricity. Finally, everything is set. Perfect. You can't see anything. I can hear that Alvise is just getting up in the other room.

I am very excited. Everything is flowing smoothly, right on schedule, as it should in a perfect crime. I double-check myself.

Italian coffee has a wonderful, stimulating aroma. Alvise loves to drink it as soon as he wakes up. I bring him a steaming cup. Then, just like a little mamma, I casually suggest a bath to him as I go out the door.

"The appointment's at nine, isn't it? I'll run you a bath. Come on, hurry up."

Then, I go back to my setup and check it once more. I turn the faucet on. It looks like a lion's head, and the powerful jet of water running from its mouth is like that of a Roman fountain.

The lion has ancient brass eyes and he seems to study me with the patience of one who is familiar with the old art of eliminating enemies and rivals.

Fortunately, water is plentiful in Rome, and the tub fills quickly, despite my impatience, which makes the time seem longer.

I peer through the steam and check the apparatus again. I am ready. I wipe away the sweat, which has grown cold despite the heat in the room.

"So? Hurry up! We'll be late. Don't we have to be at the villa at nine?"

My voice sounds a bit strained. But it's okay. In fact, Alvise comes out of the room yawning, with some newspapers under his arm, trailing the belt of his white robe which makes him look like an ancient prophet.

"Yes, I'll be right there. You know, it's really true that Rome is an Oriental city. There's something here that makes you feel like letting yourself go, forgetting everything."

Just as he enters the hall, I put the plug into the socket. From that moment on, the inviting bathtub of steaming, purifying water is the sneering instrument of my vengeance.

I clench my teeth and try to smile. I think it's a grimace, but luckily Alvise isn't looking at me. He yawns. He avidly scans the always incredible, scandalous, terrifying headlines of the Italian newspapers.

He walks past me. I breathe in his body odor for a moment. Naturally, he smells fresh and perfumed.

Wouldn't you know it, the door closes behind his back.

I am as tense as a violin string. Giddy, I go and check behind the bathroom door. I press my ear against it. Then, I watch the seconds on my watch.

I stand there, breathing heavily. Cold beads of sweat form on my forehead, and my scalp is crawling. Just then, my ball-breaking critical superego, always ready to take advantage of my moments of extreme tension, begins to taunt me and makes me feel paranoid.

"Mediocre protagonist of a second-rate mystery."

It insults me and enrages me, but nevertheless it fills my mind with logical and derogatory thoughts.

"What does Madame Euterpe say? 'He let out a blood-curdling scream.' Or, 'With a horrifying shudder that doubled him over, his body was shaken by the deadly waves of electric shock. His mouth dropped open in a mute cry, as if the fatal charge had paralyzed his vocal cords. His face was contorted in that terrible mute grimace. His blue, swollen, quivering tongue slid out between his purple lips.' Disgusting!"

"Go ahead, jeer. When I end up the victor, you'll have to admit that I've fought the good fight." But the long silence behind the door beings to worry me.

What could have happened? It's true that he could have suffered the shock in silence. It is also true that his EEG could go flat a few seconds after the shock.

"You better check it out, you piddling Cain-Iago. Fifteen minutes have already gone by, right?" Yes! Yes!! Perhaps he's already gone! Christ! The thought of Alvise's EEG going flat sends ripples of pleasure through me. People may take LSD, mescaline, and other crap like that, but there's no drug as powerful and hallucinogenic as vengeance by murder! Try and shoot up a nice hit of bloody vengeance, and you'll see what a trip it is!

Immediately, I fall into a state of rapture, with visions! I see myself dressed in Salome's veils, dancing through the sitting room and hallways, down to the kitchen.

A silver platter lies on top of the refrigerator, and on that silver platter lies Alvise's head, his eyes fixed on me.

I twirl around in my silk scarves that flutter like butterfly wings. I, the perfidious Salome, pinch his cheek and laugh. Then, I sway my hips languidly and continue my dance amid the tinkling of beads, bells and coins!

I dance back through the hallway. I am a dreamlike, ethereal, royal dancing girl as I glide back into the sitting room.

"Yeah, you're worse than a fourth-rate transvestite from the Bronx. Hey, what a supercriminal mind. Yecch!"

Ball-buster! As if one could possibly control one's own fantasies. In any case, perhaps because of the supercritic, the fantasy is over.

Sweating and upset, I stand motionless by the sideboard. Tense, I gaze at my watch. Then, I run on my tiptoes down the corridor, to the bathroom door.

I wait silently, with all my hairs standing on end, full of tics, tense and silent. Then I decide. I have to take a look. The waiting has become unbearable.

I place my hand on the doorknob and . . .

The door flies open and bashes my face in.

Alvise flings the door open and runs out to get dressed in a hurry.

The door has sent me sprawling to the floor with a Herculean uppercut.

"Oh, my God, Sammy. I'm so sorry. But what in the world were you doing behind the door? I'm really sorry. Did you get hurt?"

"No."

My nose is gushing blood, like the mouth of the traitorous lion. Yes, a traitor, because this cannot be explained.

Despite the agonizing pain in my nose, I have to know what happened.

"But, did you take your bath?"

Alvise helps me back to my feet and affectionately dabs at my nose with his robe.

"Yes, I did. In fact, thanks to you, the water was hot."

So? What happened? Why didn't it work? Alvise finally comes out with the explanation.

"Right, because if you hadn't run my bath beforehand, the water would have been cold. The strike began at eight-thirty. Didn't you see the newspaper? It's known as a wildcat strike. That's the way the Italians do it— they're always original."

A half hour later, the cardinal's big black car is driving us to the Castelli Romani, up the hill where the prelate's villa rises.

We drive through a pair of elaborate wrought-iron gates covered with coats of arms, scrolls and angels. A long boulevard lined with century-old trees runs

through a boundless park full of fantastic fountains, dazzling waterfalls and naughty marble gods and goddesses
dancing and prancing on the lawn. The whole place is
enough to make the creators of Las Vegas sick with envy.
An enormous, magnificent villa reclines regally in the
midst of this dreamlike setting. It is a miracle of marble,
columns and imposing architectural design. Alvise is familiar with its entire history—the dates of construction,
the three architects, the landscape artists, the Popes and
their families, the relatives and the coats of arms. He
rattles off all the information as if he were reading from
an open book. It makes me grind my teeth in irritation.
I already hate him today, because of the humiliating
experience in the bathroom, with the strike and all, but
now my hatred is churning stronger than ever. And
because of the door in my face, I now have to put up with
a swollen red *schnoz*, deformed by a wad of cotton stuffed
up one nostril. It hurts like hell and I feel monstrous. I
am in no condition to cope with anything. Every time
Alvise's fresh, clean fragrance wafts over to me, it is like
rubbing salt in my wounds.

I am completely mortified. So "Tell me about it, Professor"—my attempt to play along while Alvise is ex-
plaining everything—doesn't sound too convincing. He is
going on about the Renaissance. Well, I've got to admit
that it is beautiful. And the inside of that house, that
villa, that royal palace, or whatever the hell it is, is also
miraculously beautiful, with its ancient, classical décor.
It has an atmosphere of high culture and power, along
with overtones of the second great Roman Empire—that
is, the still-reigning empire of the Church Militant.

I'll omit the corridors, staircases, loggias and marble columns, which would take up forty pages of description, and get right to the dazzling dining table which is strewn with valuables of the first water: a Venetian lace tablecloth, Baccarat crystal, richly engraved silverware, exquisite gold objects and premium vintage wines.

On the walls hang paintings of royal prelates. With the patience that power bestowed on them, they watch their successors in the tail end of the speediest of centuries, the so-called modern age, gobbling the cardinal's repast.

Oh, the rival "Ineffable" of Christianity—He whose name and surname are uttered all too freely—must have had definite ideas throughout the centuries on the problem regarding *to have* and *to be*. Everything, from the lace tablecloth down to the silk stockings worn by His Eminence, emits a radiant glow. Quality, elegance, style and luxury. It all has little in common with the fisherman's friend, that carpenter's son from Galilee known as J.C., unless the chronicles have concealed the refined tendencies of that well-known group of Palestinians, also known as the superstar apostles, throughout the centuries for figurative art, literature, philosophy, the social sciences and publicity. We may not know it, but J.C. and Company, Ltd, although poor, must have been terrible snobs, and in reality, maybe even hated the vulgar cut of the toga worn by Pontius Pilate, that boorish Roman hick.

These thoughts run through my mind as I sit beneath a sixteenth-century painting of Christ at the foot of the cross. I stare at him. Handsome. Blond. Gentle. With all those fishermen friends . . .

A clap of thunder rumbles through the air and makes the crystal tremble.

I get scared and almost choke. It's clear. The Christ in the painting has his eye on me.

All right. All right. But "He whose name cannot be uttered," God of the Jews, has to understand that if I am being funny about J.C., I am also doing it for the cause. Right?

A bit of mud-slinging against competitors is an acceptable aspect of business, and is even legally permitted.

Another clap of thunder. I look at the Christ again, and then at the sky.

All right, all right. There's no need to get nervous. It's too bad for you, "Ineffable one whose name cannot be uttered"! You wanna know why? That little blond-haired guy from Nazareth is a genius, and the people adore him, literally adore him. Did you ever look at the profits made by *Jesus Christ Superstar?* Yeah, and what's more, if you really want me to spill the beans, tell me, has Zeffirelli made a film about you? No! In any case, it would be rather difficult, with your funny ideas about publicity and billboards. You'd make a lot of fuss. Would you sell your name for a brand name, for example? Just try and think about it, something like—Elohim Jeans! Well? Yeah, sure! You . . .

You're against icons, portraits and personifications. So continue being an abstraction. But don't be surprised at the slump in religious vocations, okay? When one doesn't want one's name mentioned . . .

More thunder. I shut my mouth. I look up.

What a touchy character. All right. Let's return to the dinner table. The conversation between Alvise and His Eminence is on the very subject of *being* and *having* which I mentioned earlier. Exactly what the State of Israel was and wanted to be at the beginning. The search for the values of life in *being*—that is, wise political, social and ecological policies, the great traditions, socialism, defense measures, flowering deserts, cornered markets, victorious struggles, kibbutzim, Nature and the community. Then, later on, oil, power and possession—the idea of *having*. Well, Alvise and His Eminence are deeply involved in the discussion. The cardinal gets heated.

"Be careful though. The times we live in have grown too materialistic. Maybe, just maybe, we're heading back to the irrational, according to the changing tides of history. If we may be permitted to indicate God's divine purpose in such terms."

Alvise smiles.

"I hope that the dissimilarities between our creeds will no longer prevent us from uniting our forces in the defense of human beings. The urgency to rediscover and defend human values should make us overcome any differences."

The cardinal gazes at Alvise with affection. It's clear that he really likes him.

Of course the cardinal likes the prophet Alvise. Why wouldn't he? He likes him so much that he can't help telling him so.

"Oh, it's a pity you're not in the Church, Alvise. You'd have made a marvelous cardinal."

I choke. I was just drinking some wine and it went

down the wrong way. Well, it's human. I begin to gag, and with my awful cough interrupt their mutual adulation. The secretary affectionately pats me on the back. The cardinal watches me until I calm down.

"Careful, Mr. Silverman. The creator of Mike Bullit is invaluable." Alvise takes advantage of the situation right away.

"Are you familiar with his books, Your Eminence?" The cardinal smiles.

"Oh, Mr. Silverman is too popular an author to be ignored. His mysteries are sold all over the world, and they're often found within our seminaries. A shepherd must know what nourishes his flock, don't you think?"

Right after dinner, the cardinal takes us for a walk through his beautiful library. There are endless shelves in endless corridors, three stories high. The bookcases are made of fine inlaid wood. I am in ecstasy. Damn, an entire shelf of thrillers and mysteries. I'm all there. The complete works of Mike Bullit. What a fine figure I cut! I am going to have to ask my publisher for a higher advance as soon as I get back to New York.

The noble figures of Alvise and the cardinal proceed through the wooden corridors of precious books, in dissertation like in antique paintings. The cardinal is surprisingly talkative.

"I'm quite fond of thrillers and mysteries, just as I am of comic books. I must confess, I have discovered that I like many aspects of popular culture. For example, I really enjoy anecdotes and jokes. They are conceived mysteriously among the people, generally by anonymous humorists, and often display human nature in an instructive light."

I suddenly feel encouraged to take part in the discussion.

"Excuse me, Your Eminence, but do you know the one about the great Jewish men? I mean the men who enlightened mankind? The great sages?"

"Tell me, tell me."

"Well, first came Moses. Illuminated on Mount Sinai, he raised his hands toward the sky to receive the laws. And gave the first great explanation of life: 'Everything comes from the heavens.' Then came the wise man, Solomon. He lowered his hands from the sky to his forehead. 'Everything comes from wisdom, from the light and justice of intelligence. Everything comes from the head.' Christ came along after a few years. He lowered his hands from his head to his heart. 'Everything is love. Love thy neighbor as thyself. Everything comes from your heart.' That worked well until Marx came around and lowered his hands from his heart to his stomach. 'Everything lies here. The true conflicts, senses, meanings and philosophies of life lie in the state of the economy. Here! Everything comes from the belly.' But a few years later came Freud. He slid his hands down further, if you'll excuse me, down to the amatory, libidinous parts. He explained that the true sense of everything originates there—Eros, Psyche, folly, art, and life and death. 'Everything is summed up there, in sex.' Finally, Einstein leapt to his feet and stopped them all. 'Careful, boys, careful. Everything is relative!' "

Everyone laughs. It is the first time in a long while

that I feel on the ball. For once, I made a good move. I mean, I could have remembered any one of the thousands of dirty jokes for which I am famous. But instead, I managed to come up with one that was . . . let's say, "pertinent."

I continue to cut a fine figure.

I meet Alvise's glowing eyes. He is pleased with me like a mother who hears the good news that her son got an excellent grade in math.

His gaze bothers me a bit, but I feel magnanimous and forgive him. His Eminence is truly amused.

"Wonderful. It's much more than an anecdote. It's a lesson in religious philosophy. It also reminds us somewhat discreetly of the great contribution that Jewish culture has made to our civilization. I'm an admirer of yours, you know. I believe that the mystery genre has given birth to some excellent writers."

Continuing his role of the proud mother, Alvise catches the ball on the rebound.

"You're absolutely right, Your Eminence. And in Sammy's case we're in for some surprises. He's been feeling a profound revulsion against this consumer society. I'm happy about that because, in reality, Sammy is a poet."

I blush.

"Oh, knock it off, Alvise."

But Alvise insists. He wants to go on talking about me, and how the consumer society forces the artist to become a whore—he uses the phrase to prostitute himself—in order to gain ephemeral possessions. He tells the cardinal how I rebelled and sought other values—the values of *being*. His Eminence ends up taking an interest in me. He asks me questions and I answer.

I gradually draw close to his armchair and, without noticing, I am squatting on a little footstool beside him. The atmosphere becomes that of the confessional. Without expressing any opinion, the cardinal grows interested in my problem as we go on chatting. He wants to know about me and the book I intend to write.

I begin to talk about my project.

It's always the same old project—the one I dreamt about doing in college when I was twenty. *A World Without Words,* a novel in verse, a figurative, semiotic journey through the language of signs and modes of communication relating to poetry.

In other words, absolute bullshit, or at least that's how I see it as I speak to him. I babble on, I let myself go, I ease off the brakes, and away I go! Like wetting the bed. I spew out some sort of confession! I don't know what the hell is coming over me.

A form of verbal diarrhea. Unable to stop myself, I unload an avalanche of bullshit for half an hour. It's like an abyss, a bottomless pit. The presence of that paternal, authoritative ear . . . I feel purged.

I can suddenly see why the Catholics spend less on psychoanalysts than the Protestants and us Jews. As for the idea of liberating speech, Mr. Freud has some considerable precedents to draw on. What is certain is that I can no longer keep my mouth shut.

I inundate the evening with words. Total logorrhea. No holding back!

*   *   *

"I don't know what the hell got into me. I made an ass out of myself."

The pavements in Rome ring hollow at night. We are going back to the apartment. We walk up the cool, spacious staircase. When we open the door, it's dark. Alvise's voice sounds suave in the darkness.

"Speaking for His Eminence, as well as for myself, you are a subject of great interest. Because of your career, because of your identity crisis, because of everything. Sammy, you're worth more than you think you are."

I try to turn on the light.

"Did you forget about the wildcat strike?"

"Oh, yeah!"

With a pang, I remember everything clearly.

"The electricity strike."

Alvise gropes his way through the living room and comes back with a lit candle. I run into something and bang my shinbone. The pain in my shinbone is now added to the pain in my nose.

Fortunately, I can laugh about it instead of crying.

"I'm drunk."

"The cardinal's wine was excellent, the dinner too."

"Yeah. But I overdid it."

I really feel that I did overdo it, and I think I better get into that bathroom before I make a mess of things.

I go in, by the trembling light of the candle. The beautiful antique tiles, the useless tub and the lion-headed faucet. They all greet me like old accomplices. I look in the mirror and see a moron. The light from the candle gives me a ghostly look. I have a mocking sneer, a swollen nose, and my eyes are glistening from all the booze. I am simply disgusting.

As I pull my pants down, I think about human misery. A failed murderer and perhaps an unsuccessful poet. A human being who is about to fulfill his destiny still has to pull down his pants and take a shit. Shit . . . a symbolic object for what our body has decided to get rid of. Shit, with it's strong, persistent odor. Prepared in elegant brown cords, it assumes a variety of forms depending on how it is excreted. The most classical form is when it is rolled with an upward twist. There are some great worshipers of this base human matter. They have an attractive name—fecologists, or something like that. It seems that there are even depraved sensualists—coprophagists —who actually eat the stuff! Now that's revolting! Feces occupy a central position in an incredible number of jokes. It's a profound, daily part of our lives. The French, who are intellectuals, even use *merde* as commas. Well, well. Thinking about the French, my attention suddenly falls on that intimate, hygienic little monument that is so lacking in the U.S.A. and the Protestant countries of the world. I mean the bidet.

You have to admit that it's very practical and hygienic. I turn the water on and pick up the newspaper that Alvise left behind this morning. Yes, reading the newspaper in the bathroom is a widespread habit that allows you to keep your head busy during that purging and humiliating duty. There is an article on the strike. Sure. You really have to be careful reading Italian newspapers. The strikes are not only varied and numerous, but they occur by fits and starts and at strange hours of the day. Unexpected or organized. They have fabulous names. If it weren't so damned annoying, it might be amusing. Ah, there. Something at the cardinal's didn't agree with me, because my corporal evacuation is violent, noisy and painful. Anyway, the lights suddenly come back on. I can read the newspaper better now, and there are a lot of things to read. Ah, Italy, what a strange, contradictory country. Alive and man-eating. Full of incredible scandals, one right after the other. The latest one has something to do with a bank fraud, of the Vatican it seems. I immerse myself in the article as I mechanically complete the operation—you know what I'm talking about. I am right in the middle of an absorbing paragraph, when I am suddenly struck by a lightning bolt hurled by "He whose name should not be uttered," but which I scream out wildly anyway, sometime after a terrible leap, and before I fall. I receive a violent electrical shock which sends me smashing against the sink across the room. My erogenous zone is sizzled by a charge of electrical current.

Alvise bursts into the bathroom. He bends over me. I am lying on the floor, screaming in agony, with my pants down to my knees. A major disaster. I am disgusting, but also pathetic.

I gaze up at him with an undefinable expression. The night, that mocking, taunting cat, sweeps its black veils around me.

When the black veils reopen, the Roman night is filled with howling sirens.
Our ambulance is speeding.

I wake up and find myself lying among the gravely wounded victims of accidents, shootings and bombings.

"He whose name cannot be uttered" is really beginning to exaggerate; Mafia, some biblical curse or black magic. Certainly, if his aim is to frighten me, he is doing a good job of it.

Alvise is at my side.

By now, I realize that he has a strong celestial connection. He obviously has an aura. Getting right down to it, there is someone pretty powerful looking after him. He must be in good with the superior power. My thoughts and scowling grimaces are interrupted. A quick slam on the brakes. Someone has laid an ambush.

The ambulance attendant is hysterical as he yells to the driver.

"Watch out! There are three guys with masked faces!"

The driver shouts back.

"It's an ambush! Get down!"

The wounded toss around on their stretchers. Most of them are only kids.

"They're those sons of bitches from the Workers' Autonomy group."

"Son-of-a-bitch yourself. I'm with the Workers' Autonomy. Cripes, they stuck us in here with a bunch of fascists!"

The wounded strain to pull themselves up.

One of the masked boys outside threatens the ambulance attendant with a machine gun until they open the doors.

The attendant pales.

"Don't open up, don't open up!"

The driver is obviously not cut out to be a hero.

"You're nuts! He's got a gun!"

The door opens and a boy with the machine gun jumps in.

"Get down, comrades. And you fuckin' fascists watch out, because I can pull this trigger any time."

There is a sudden tumult in the ambulance when many of the wounded try to crawl out. Alvise heads for the door, irresistibly drawn by his destiny as a prophet.

"Bravo! Good idea pointing a machine gun. You could blow out quite a few brains here. They're all wounded and can't defend themselves."

The masked terrorist with the gun gets angry.

"Mind your own fuckin' business, shithead, Capitalist pig, murderer."

Others react. Alvise tries to stop things once again. He speaks above the uproar in his melodious voice.

"Would you let a so-called shithead who won't mind his own business ask you something?"

"No!"

The terrorist suddenly hits him over the head with the butt of his machine gun. Alvise falls to the ground.

The terrorist fires a round of shots into the air which makes the operation proceed at a quick speed. I lift myself from the stretcher and watch everything.

Well! After so much suffering, this is a moment of pure joy. Someone finally hit that haloed head, and shut the prophet's mouth.

As I rejoice over that moment of bliss, things begin

to get complicated. A battle is raging among the wounded.

One of the injured happens to have a gun. Shots are fired. No one understands how or why or what is going on.

And I, for the first time in almost a month since my life has been turned upside down, feel a new sense of serenity.

Alvise is stretched out on the ground, motionless. My joy also contains a ray of hope. Alvise is so still. Could it be that after so many bad jokes, "He whose name cannot be uttered" has decided to grant my petition?

The remote hope that Alvise is dead, combined with a brilliant flash of inspiration, gives me the impetus to start making definite plans for my new book. I know it sounds incredible, but it's true. *A World Without Words* is conceived in that moment of grace, during that battle.

Marrakesh! Surprise! How did Marrakesh suddenly come in, city of caravans, with its Arab markets and belly dances? What relationship could there be between the palms swaying in the perfumed desert wind and the flaming eyes beneath the Tuareg women's mysterious veils—and the Roman ambulance in the midst of a battle and Alvise knocked down by urban guerrillas?

The Ineffable, whose name I pronounce in vain, has his inscrutable ways. The only sure thing is that, along these ways leading me to Marrakesh, on a nonstop direct flight, Alvise sits by my side, alive and thriving. In fact, I can see Marrakesh from the plane. It's a beautiful Arab city. We dance a waltz in the sky over the softly swelling cupolas of the minarets. I sit there with bandages over my privates. By the way, everything seems fine—all I'd need would be to end up impotent as a fitting finale for this adventure. Instead, in a few days' time I shall have the doctor's permission to commit impure acts. Alvise, of course, only has a little Band-Aid on his forehead. Wouldn't you just know it!

He's hardly bruised at all. Amnesty International, after what happened in Iran and the hostages affair, after the peace between Egypt and Israel, after the Ethiopian-Somalian conflicts, after the interventions of Qaddafi, who's suspected by now of everything and anything, after Afghanistan, Pakistan and the myriad hotbeds of violence in Africa and Asia, and the thousand turmoils of Islam, has decided to hold a demonstration against the violence of the Arab world. So, the prophet of *being* and of nonviolence is flying to convey his message in the heart of Morocco.

My glassy eyes slide indifferently over the round bellies of the minarets.

My identity crisis has grown deeper than ever after my latest experiences.

Anyway, I do not intend to act as the perpetual appendix to the perfect superprophet Alvise-Isaac in his wanderings. For me, Marrakesh is the last chance—*"le dernier métro,"* as the French would say. The last occasion to have it, I mean Alvise's head. If I fail even this time, I'll throw in the towel, I'll declare a forfeit, I'll give up. Full stop, and a new paragraph. You gotta know how to lose.

I'll go back to old New York, to Alice . . . and to my destiny as a second-rate writer.

Strangely enough, though, this decision, along with the defeats I've suffered recently, does not placate my desire for justice. Justice, yes! Because *mors tua vita mea!* Because it has now become a question of principle, also in regard to "He whose name cannot be uttered." I look down at the minarets, thinking: In my gloomy story, what better background would there be, for a finale, than a fabulous Moroccan city?

Marrakesh welcomes us right away, with its exciting mysteries, its lights and its jagged shadows.

As soon as we leave the airport, we go to an Arab market.

A bazaar is really something! We are wrapped up by the beauty of the Moroccan world, full of crowds, booths, sunlight, vendors' cries, colors shining among blinding whites, the sounds of repetitive sensual instruments, beards, misery, veiled women, and all the rest, which lay under the bright glare of the tents obscuring the sunny sky.

Alvise and I walk through the crowds.

Just like in a movie. Arab markets that would make Hitchcock drool! I get many ideas for thrillers in that place.

Alvise and I get along well in that colorful confusion of the Orient. We look like one of those ambiguous Anglo-Saxon tourist couples who populate those hospitable regions full of palms and Tuaregs.

The women's black eyes watch us through their rags with curiosity. They give the impression of being truly repulsive beneath their veils, which are really some type of ridiculous handkerchiefs.

I pause in front of a merchant who's crouched on the ground over a rag where he has his goods exhibited. It's just a little pile of yellow stones, which may be myrrh, and a stained pen-holder, some broken glasses and a rusty spoon.

"Jesus, this guy's in competition with Macy's. No, let me try to understand. How can this guy make a living with this kind of trade? Is he doing it for a hobby?"

Alvise takes some money out of his pocket.

Well, that's another typical reaction, which I find extremely irritating: For every country we visit, he always has the right kind of money, and knows exactly how much it's worth. He throws two coins to the old man.

"You don't realize what depths misery can reach. There are people who actually die of starvation here. And don't forget that they've got oil in this land. And still, the social situation of the African countries . . ."

I look at Alvise with imploring eyes.

"Chief, please, be kind. I'm really very interested in the social political situation in Africa, I swear it. But let's just take a nice little tourist's walk. God! This exotic atmosphere is so exciting! Tomorrow, at the demonstration, I'll be listening. I promise. But right now, please, just lay off the social problems a bit. I'd like to see a harem! You know, it's my first time here! I feel some sort of strange, languid, restless charm. I don't know, it seems like anything could happen here. Is there any hope of being kidnapped by a female sheik?"

Alvise laughs.

"Don't start dreaming, Sammy. There's only work to be done here. You on your book and me in my meetings. Still, you're right, this place has got a sensuality that you just breathe in, together with a sense of mystery. White walls, eyes staring at you . . . and the desert that calls. *Mal d'Afrique.* Just wait till you see the house we're staying in. Mazarin is in London and he's lending us the 'Sultana.' You'll love it. It's an enchanted place. It used to belong to a great, wise sheik who wrote fabulous fairy tales there. It's a fantastic place for working and meditating. You'll see, you'll love it."

You can bet your ass that I'll love it! It's some kind of Mohammed's paradise. I mean, you get it? The Sultana.

Palm trees, fountains, flowers, little birds, Moroccan splendors of marquetry and majolica. The beautiful villa is a Moorish dream.

An azure swimming pool, as large as Lake Ontario, sparkles with jeweled drops of water in the blinding sunlight.

Moroccan servants bow to us. No doubt. It's the Mohammedan paradise.

And he, I mean, Alvise, is as happy there as a worm on a lettuce leaf.

He looks like a prince in his fine white and beige linen suit.

He speaks with the servants, who already look at him with affection and enchantment. He's the "good white master," or perhaps even more. I'm watching him from a mullioned window, with mixed feelings of fascination and irritation.

Look how they genuflect! Who the hell is he?! The

Prince of Wales? Or perhaps "Allah is great, Mohammed is his prophet," and Alvise is the Prophet's prophet?!

He doesn't even sweat, damn him. I sure am sweating though, fanning myself with a palm leaf. Alvise looks up at my window.

"Hey, Sammy! Are you settled? Did you notice what your room is called?"

"I thought you called it a room. Why, do they have a special name for it here?"

"Just look around."

Curiously, I look around my room. It's splendid. Full of Moorish fretwork and marquetry. There is an enormous, low sofa bed close to the floor, covered with a heap of cushions.

On one wall, in the midst of the frescoes, I notice a painting.

It's an old watercolor done in a kind of Moorish art-nouveau style. Just guess what it's about! Well, yes! It's Salome's dance! With my eyes popping out, I draw closer and read the inscription beneath it: *La Danse de Salomé*.

Strauss's music explodes loudly in my ears.

A swirling mist of veils and iridescent pearls. This time, all of Strauss's art-nouveau languor and sensuality magically swell the air during the performance of the princess's dance. Yes! There she is! The lethal Princess Salome. With all her seven veils, and the force of symbol and destiny working through her, she dances before the tetrarch and her lustful mother, Herodias, in order to execute her vengeance and obtain the prophet's head.

The notes of the music waft through the air. On the podium stands the handsome, charming, slightly withered Maestro von Kramer, directing the orchestra with passion.

Yes. Events follow one another at an alarming pace! Portents of destiny . . . That in the heart of Morocco there is a theater, and that in this theater they're performing my very own *Salomé,* and that Salome also happens to be the name of my room in the Sultana: All these coincidences unleash a growing tension within me. There is no doubt about it. It's like the children's game "Hot and Cold." I'm getting hotter. I'm drawing closer to the magic moment.

Everything that happened before was only a warm-up! We're in the hot center of the story. How and when shall I succeed in doing my dance? I'm ready to seize the right moment.

Alvise has calmly stood almost fifty hours of debate on the themes "Oil and Violence—the price of growth in the African continent" and "Does the great Islam belong to Qaddafi, Arafat, Khomeini or the sheiks?" That kind of lecture was enough to kill an ox. I was already gasping for air after half an hour of that crap. And now he's very relaxed, I mean Alvise, the guest of honor of the Institute of Moroccan Culture. He's enjoying the theatrical performance, looking as fresh as a daisy. The conductor also happens to be an old friend of his.

Of course, we are in the box reserved for the authorities, sitting among Arab and European dignitaries.

"We absolutely must go and greet von Kramer after

the performance," Alvise whispers in my ear. "Ten years have passed since we last saw each other. He's a great artist and a great friend."

I watch the maestro conducting the orchestra. His lean, tense figure is exquisitely neurotic. Salome is dancing in front of the prophet. Something makes me feel uneasy, something strange is floating in the air. I don't know what it is.

That feeling is still with me as we head for the dressing rooms. We elbow our way through the colorful crowd.

On the stage, the company is receiving applause, congratulations and flowers. Alvise and Franz von Kramer embrace each other warmly.

I watch them and continue to feel that uneasy sensation, a sort of alarming itch.

It's an authentic meeting of old friends. They look into each other's eyes and smile with nostalgia. I happen to be standing near the Salome of the performance. She doesn't know it, but I feel as if I were meeting a member of my family. I take advantage of her admirers' embraces and compliments, and touch her veil, making her little bells jingle. When she notices my excessive familiarity, she gives me a dirty look. I kiss her hand, and then drag her over to Alvise and von Kramer so as to cover up my strange behavior.

Alvise kisses her hand too.

It's a great success. Von Kramer is the celebrated star —I slither away through the crowds, and find myself in a sea of male dancers dressed as warriors, veiled maidens, golden glitter, hieroglyphics and serpentine eyes like Nefertiti's.

And yet, in the midst of the celebrations, the compliments, the autographs and the flowers, von Kramer slips away. It's odd. That magic moment that follows a successful performance is usually sacred for an artist. Why does von Kramer want to slink away instead? Where could he hide himself? By chance, I happen to see him running in the wings: He has an unhappy, grim expression on his pale face. He disappears behind the stage door without looking back.

Alvise is searching for him in the crowd. I wink at him: The maestro has left, he's gone, I saw him.

Alvise grabs me and drags me toward the stage door.

Maybe something dramatic occurred in the midst of all the confusion. But we are the only ones who have noticed von Kramer's disappearance. The celebration of the première carries on full force.

Alvise is upset. He's insensitive to the hunger pangs that always follow theatrical performances and to the sensuous aromas of jasmine that waft over to us from the nearby residential gardens. He hails a taxi instead.

"Hey, where are we going? You don't even know where he went? Anyway, if he left, it means he had things to do. Let's go to dinner with the company. Maybe he'll meet us there later."

"No. I don't like him running off like that. Maybe I shouldn't have come to see him. You don't know, there are old stories . . . Maybe I upset him. But his running off like this tonight . . . I don't like it. If he ran away like that, it means he's out of his mind. We've got to find him immediately. When he's in one of these moods, he's capable of anything."

And he drags me into the belly of an Oriental taxi full of little carpets, altars, gold fringe, plastic bayadère dancers and an unbearable jasmine deodorant. Hey, did I say "belly"? Yes, the belly of the taxi.

I didn't say the word "belly" just by chance. It must have been some sort of omen, I think as I watch the gyrating, swirling belly of an expert Moroccan dancing girl. We are sitting on the floor on uncomfortable cushions. All the same, what a dance it is! Vibrant quiverings of all the flesh surrounding her navel. It's the ancient art, it's the cry of the gypsy dancers, of the little Tuareg girls who follow the caravans across the desert, of the women belonging to the caravanseries, where life, food, survival or total slavery depend on the sheik's whims.

Our stripteasers, who swing little chains and diamond pendants from their tits, tushies and depilated pussies, are pathetic in comparison! I mean, the art of belly dancing could only have been brought to such perfection under the threat of torture and terror.

I sit crouched on the ground along with the other spectators. Low, little tables in front of us. My circulation is blocked in one calf and my eyes are bulging as if I had fallen into a trance, watching those gyrating bellies and swirling veils. I even feel my orangutan waking up. Yes, because with all those explosive Israelis and terroristic Romans, well, there hasn't been any available sex since back there with Alice the wifey.

The Arab music is growing cacophonous and frenetic, and it suddenly pops into my head that the crazy dancer who keeps undulating her trembling little belly is in some ways a Salome too, or at least one of her schoolmates.

Salome. Salome the inspirer. Salome, the patron saint. Salome, the muse. Salome, the goddess of vengeance.

Yeah. Everything is written in the Book of Destiny. *"Mek tub"*—everything is written—is what they say around here.

Dazzling and powerful as she was, Salome felt like shit soon after she met Saint John the Baptist. That's how it goes. I understand how you feel, dear little sister Salome. I know what kind of hate—true, pure hate—perfection inspires.

Has there ever been anything closer than you and me, little princess? Your myth is already written and famous, mine is yet to be accomplished.

And wasn't Fate bizarre to place you there, over the head of Alvise playing the violin in front of me in Venice, the very first day we all met. Me, my prophet and my destiny?

Alvise joins me through the crowd of drunken American and German tourists and the androgynous, semi-nude boys acting as waiters.

"No. He hasn't been seen yet, but I'm sure that he'll be here."

"Why? Did he tell you he'd come here?"

"No, but this is a well-known place. It's a club which

has great literary traditions, Oscar Wilde has been here, and Gide . . ."

In the middle of the stage, behind her veils, the girl is shaking her belly, buttocks, thighs and breasts more and more intensely. I look around at the tourists. They are all men. No, wait a minute. I take a closer look.

Many of the little Arab serving girls are actually young boys.

But even the audience is largely composed of classic queens who'd come all the way to Morocco to get their "back doors banged"!

At once, the truth flashes inside me.

Of course. Elementary, my dear Watson.

"Ah! A case of *No, No, Nanette*—'All the nice boys love sailors.' That's what our maestro is: a fag!"

I laugh. Alvise, worried and affectionate, wants me to view dear Franz's problem in a civilized *und* Freudian manner.

"A beloved mother who spoiled him and prevented him from becoming a man. A brilliant talent that made everybody immediately adore him. That's what perpetuated his exclusive relationship with his mother. He was given everything. Success, art, love . . . and beauty. Therefore, he was condemned to solitude and fragility. Poor Franz. He's such a good man, yet he suffers like a beast. Poor Franz. Poor thing. Beauty, success, talent, love . . ."

Sure, what a drag. The more Alvise talks, the more my balls revolve with supersonic speed. I mean, what are we to do? Burst into tears? Tear our hair out? Pray and make burnt offerings to the Ineffable? For this heart-breaking tragedy that made crow's-feet appear on poor Franz? I mean, after all—it's just a matter of a poor old pansy going through menopause, right? A wrinkled old queen in search of thrills. Alvise is really going too far this time. To keep from bursting out with one of those healthy vulgar fits that comfort me in times of anger, I drop the matter and go back to watching the show.

Yeah, because before I had to hear about the painful story of poor little Franzine, I had been watching that tasty Morocco morsel shaking her devilish little cooker. My convalescent orangutan had been perking up a little.

After all, I had a medical permit to go back into action. And I was just about to. But sudden crankiness can play nasty tricks on you.

Soon I realize that my orangutan, which had raised its head at the sight of the nice little Moroccan belly, has now settled down with detached interest after hearing about "Poor Franz." By this time, I'm pretty pissed off. Dammitall! The beast is supposed to sustain the honor of the flag, as well as the pole itself! And you never know. With all this running around for vengeance and rescue operations, one can end up losing the healthy habits of certain pleasures, which only amount to three or four, after all. I wouldn't like to add this onto Alvise's already spicy account. I lay into him.

"This Arab broad sure is a knockout. Look how she gets into it with that little belly of hers! Boy, if that's the way she dances, I wonder how she . . . Must have some great techniques, huh?"

Alvise looks bored.

"It's just a show for drunken tourists."

"And what am I? A drunken tourist, right."

I get up and go dancing with the little Arab girl.

I act like a clumsy, vulgar idiot, worse than a giddy soldier on leave. I even try to imitate her belly dance.

Who knows why, but when I offend Alvise with my deliberate, exaggerated vulgarity, I feel almost a sense of pleasure. Yes, I like it. I enjoy it, like that time in Venice, when I was a child, when I told him about the Jews escaping with diamonds up their bums.

"Just say it. Say it, little lord. Tell me that you find me vulgar. Have the courage to face up to your aristocratic, super-refined snotty-nosed snobbery. Get a load of my belly dance, and my sweaty armpits, my pubic bumps and grinds, and my swaying hips. As you can see, old pal, the audience is going simply wild for my performance."

The audience applauds and whistles in the end. Instead of going back to my place, I slip through the curtains after the Arab girl and disappear before everyone's eyes—especially before yours, dear Alvise.

The back of the club is squalid and full of rags like a junk shop, loaded with gypsy bedouin odds and ends. Instead of walls, the corridors and dressing rooms consist of curtains and draperies.

The sweating little Arab girl slides through a gap between two curtains. I follow her.

Her little space of colorful clothes has a mirror. Veils and costumes covered with little gold medals are scattered here and there. The brunette turns around, sees that I've slipped in and giggles beneath her veil.

Hold it, stop everything. Quiet. Quiet for a while.

The convalescent patient is sending out messages. The survivor of the great electrical bidet is giving intermittent signals. Yes, yes, yes, yes. The orangutan is showing signs of interest again. That sexual appendage—the bull, the condor, the Viking, the gorilla, the scimitar, the sword, the sledgehammer, the saber, the devil's blessed shaft—after so many awful experiences and a long period of lethargy, is finally sitting up and begging. It was all Alvise's fault. He'd make even Don Juan give up, and would drive Casanova to sign up for Amnesty International.

Anyway, the little Arab chocolate morsel has quite a few nice curves, and an appetizing animal smell. The orangutan gets ready for battle, hardens, wakes up and raises its head.

She is very, very young, with a nice slender waist and pert little tits. She has a cute, squealing laugh, the provocative little minx, but then she removes her veil, and reveals an ugly gap-toothed mouth that immediately turns her into a witch, just like in the jokes. The orangutan suddenly drops his fantasy, but the Arab girl doesn't know it and goes right on flirting.

"Monsieur a envie de s'amuser cette nuit, n'est-ce pas?"

I give her a stupid grin and slump down on a footstool. I'm still breathing heavily from the belly dance. But I've decided to waste some time in that hole just to vex the superman outside, hoping he'll think the worst.

I sigh and begin to joke with the girl.

"Eh . . . Pourquoi pas? Ton nom?"

"Fatima."

And she smiles with that black gaping hole in her

mouth. You just can't grasp how anyone could want to make her do it—smile, I mean, for goodness sake! I mean, you've got an orthodontic mess like that, you should keep your mouth shut, right? Let's just forget about it, Fatima. Anyway, I decide to play along to gain some time.

"*Mmmmm! Joli nom, Fatima.*"

Just then, a huge, fat Arab wearing a fez walks in. I don't know if he is her father or her pimp, the only sure thing is that he gives me a dirty look, and I start getting nervous.

The huge Arab spits out a volley of words that I don't understand. Could it be possible that in this sleazy Moroccan hole, the girls are all vestal virgins? Maybe this guy is the big brother who likes beating people up! It is not likely, since the girl began undressing. Sure, after jabbering with her for quite a while, the fat guy turns to me, makes a little bow and gets down to business.

"Monsieur, you want belly dance private, eh?"

"It depends."

"Fatima is little flower. Fifty dollars."

You get that? They go light on foreigners. And with my fingers held together, I tap the Arab guy's forehead to make him understand that I think he's off his rocker.

"You're nuts! Fifty bucks, and she's even toothless. Send her to a dentist first, okay?"

And I walk out of that place of sin for assholes. Behind my back, I can hear the two babbling away in Arabic. The fat guy sounds nervous, the girl is shrieking. In the shadows, I make my way through the hanging drapes and head back to the main room, where the red lights and music are in full swing. I can glimpse the stage through a small gap. Alvise is watching the show with an unusual degree of attention. I'm surprised to see him so absorbed with the dancer, when he had seemed so bored before. But then I notice that the dancer is not female but male. It's some kind of young boy with rounded feminine limbs, a graceful ephebe, who is dancing the belly dance quite a lot better than Fatima had done. He's so made up he looks like an overpainted whore.

A cruel smile pulls at the corners of my lips.

"Well? What's that intense look for? What? The little Arab girl with the frolicking tush and the lively navel was just cheap crap for tourists, but this little faggot here makes the whole thing a lot more interesting?" This thought makes its way through my head and gives a new tinge to my relationship with the super-perfect prophet. And it begins to twist and dig like a worm. Right. After all, why not?

My cruel smile stretches my sardonic lips even more. A mixed look of ironic contempt and great hope shines in my eyes and my heart. Could Alvise be a faggot?

I remember Dorothea's words exactly. They are blood-red flashing neon lights in my mind. "Who knows what Alvise sees in you? He adores you. He really has a crush on you." Of course! That's it. That explains everything. Dorothea, Maestro Franz, and yes, me too. It's too beautiful to be true.

"Oh, God, God of the oceans and of the heavens, great and terrible Adonai, cast your fateful eye on your servant Sammy. Oh, dammitall, sorry, I fell for it again. I uttered your name. Sorry. 'He whose name shall never more be uttered,' forgive me and assist me. Oh, please let Alvise be a faggot, and let him be passionately in love with me. And that I, stupid asshole that I am, blinded by my complexes, didn't realize it.

"Let him be a pansy, a homo, a queer, a faggot, a queen, a fairy, a fruitcake, a pederast, a sodomite, a sado-masochist, an invert, a stretched out asshole . . . I beg you, oh 'Ineffable, whose name cannot be uttered.' "

A turmoil, an agitated muttering of broken, incomprehensible words of Arabic dialects. Something behind one of the many curtains down at the end of the dark corridor seizes my attention. I think I hear a low, dramatic voice sobbing out a few words in English. I'm as curious as the proverbial cat and I can't resist. Of course you should mind your own business. It's true. Especially in some kind of an Oriental cathouse with no locks, let alone doors. But something lures me irresistibly.

The big Arab guy passes by, looking upset.

Then a fat old woman walks by with two androgynous little waiters.

All this traffic leads down to the curtain in the back.

Nobody notices me in the shadows, so I go over to cast a furtive glance among the colorful rags.

An ugly dressing room, like Fatima's. A sort of sofa made up of filthy rags and cushions. Maestro von Kramer is there, kneeling down in a biblical attitude, or —since I don't know of anybody in the Bible having his forehead down and his ass pointing to the stars—let's say sheepstyle. He's held there by a large, mustached Arab male whore in his shorts. Something red is dripping down. Christ! Von Kramer is bleeding at the wrists.

I nearly have apoplexy, dammitall. It's obvious the maestro is raving to be left to die. He's insulting that poor mustached body-vendor, that honest male hooker, who's completely ignorant of the existential crises of a European artist.

Actually, von Kramer, who is either stoned, on a bad trip, drunk out of his mind or sick in the head, looks like a beast. Though the young stud tries to silence him by stopping his mouth against his thigh, the maestro still manages to roar out:

"Let me die, you ugly Arab slut! I'm my own master! I want to die. Take the money and get out of here."

Though the fine, upstanding mustached whore may not understand, he doesn't let him off all the same. He tightens and holds the lacerated wrists up high, trying to stop the streaming blood.

I shake myself out of my daze and rush to the main room.

Through the curtains, I catch a glimpse of the lascivious male dancer still shaking his feminine hips feverishly.

I wave desperately, trying to get Alvise's attention. He doesn't see me. Then I blow a shrill whistle with my fingers. Fortunately, there is so much noise that the other tourists do not notice a thing.

Alvise finally sees me. I'm waving at him wildly. He gets up, drawn by my frenetic gesticulating.

"It's the maestro. Come on, quick."

Alvise turns white. That was what he had feared all

along. He rushes down the corridor, with me close behind.

He bursts into the dressing room. Franz is writing like a madman. The poor, honest mustached whore happily welcomes the end of his responsibility.

Quick, clever and without a word, Alvise takes his place.

"Franz, calm down. I'm here now."

Franz is panic-stricken.

"Oh, no! Alvise, no. I beg you, no. Not you."

I watch in a stupor as Alvise hands me Franz's wrists, snatches the precious silk Hermès scarf from my neck and swiftly rips it into strips with his teeth.

The sight of blood always upsets me, I've said it before, but I suffer even more when I see Alvise tearing the scarf before my very eyes. That scarf was a fantasy of forest greens, just like the color of my eyes. Oh, well!

With his great surgical technique, Alvise quickly puts temporary bandages around the maestro's wrists. Franz looks at him. He stops struggling, defeated, weak, hallucinating, delirious.

"Why do you want to hold me back? I don't ever want to go back to Vienna. I don't want anyone anymore. I came here to hit the bottom and die. It's time for the end to come. I wanted it to have the face, body and bestiality of these dark, mustached studs. It's the kind of end I like. I lived well. I want to die well. Don't get involved, my friend."

Alvise is tender, yet strong and firm. His hands work quickly, as he glances affectionately at his friend.

"Please. The idea of old age disgusts me. It always

has. I hate it. I can't bear it. My sagging flesh horrifies me. I want my death to be beautiful. I can't look at ugliness. Don't interfere. If only I had Rimbaud's strength, I'd trade young slaves . . . And who's this?"

Franz suddenly becomes aware of my presence. I smile at him uncertainly.

"Hello."

Alvise intervenes immediately.

"Sam Silverman. You met him before at the theater."

Franz looks bitter and skeptical. He whispers in his weakness, casting me a suspicious, disillusioned look.

"Treacherous sluts."

I look at Franz and then at Alvise, embarrassed.

"Let's get out of here before they call the police."

"Just a bunch of ugly, treacherous cunts."

Well, he goes on with the insults. Not bad. A lot of crap from a pathetic old faggot. In this situation, Alvise is as serene and enigmatic as an egg. He doesn't move a muscle at the insults, something which I, at this point, find intriguing and unsettling! New perspectives. He keeps babbling.

"Stinking, wornout sluts. Scumbags."

I finally get pissed! What the hell!

"Maestro, if there's a whore or a cunt around here, it's *you!*"

Alvise looks at me severely.

"Sammy, what are you saying? He's out of his mind. He's full of booze and drugs, and half drained of his blood. How can you?"

"He's the one who started it."

We finally take him to the hospital. We make it just

in time. They treat him and he is out of danger. Before dawn, they give us permission to take him away, so as to avoid any possibility of scandal.

Maestro von Kramer looks ravaged when he is brought out of the emergency room. Alvise smiles and tries to cheer up his friend.

"I'm in the mood for a cup of steaming coffee with hot milk. There are probably already fresh croissants at this hour. It's almost dawn. You always liked croissants. Remember, in Paris?"

Von Kramer now appears really old and tired. He is pale, and his eyes are full of tears.

"I didn't want you to see me this way, Alvise. You, of all people. You . . . What a joke! Paris. Jesus Christ. When we were in our twenties . . . Those marvelous, wretched, overwhelming, crazy years . . ."

At the end of the hall, there is a mirror. Franz unfortunately happens to see his reflected image. He stops. Stiffening, he frees himself from our protective arms. Watching him cautiously, Alvise lets him face the test.

I feel a bit embarrassed. The tragedy of the aging faggot. I'm not prejudiced, but, I mean, really . . . I don't give a damn. Or, to put it more colorfully: Hey, what the fuck! So, I watch the famous Maestro von Kramer rather indifferently as he slowly approaches the mirror, touching his wrecked face with his hands. Eyes sagging with wrinkles, cracked mouth, green skin and white hair. Just like Garbo. No, sorry, Greta—you at least carry your old age with great class.

Alvise stands by him.

"You've never been more attractive, Franz. You don't

have to believe that, since you're such a hedonist. But suffering suits you."

Von Kramer isn't listening. He gazes at himself with desperation and then suddenly winces in horror.

Like a wounded animal, he darts toward the window at the end of the hallway.

Alvise runs after him. After a moment of uncertainty, I follow.

We both cling to the aspiring suicide who is trying to climb over the parapet. The maestro shrieks:

"*Auf Wiedersehen,* Alvise. *Tout est fini!* Or *tutto finiii!*"

Alvise later tells me that "*tutto fini*" is the last line of Violetta's opening aria in the final act of *La Traviata,* the opera version of *La Dame aux Camélias.*

I haven't even registered this fact, because the struggle is dangerous and unbalancing. Alvise manages to hold Franz back, but blocks him in such a way that it is I who lose my balance. Being pushed a bit by the outburst on the ledge and also by Franz's kicking, I find myself wildly waving my arms like a windmill. Then . . .

"Oh, my God! Son-of-aaaaa . . ."

I fall off the ledge.

Fortunately, it's on the second floor, and the old Marrakesh hospital, a converted colonial building, faces out on a little alley where a morning market is just coming to life, in the first glimmerings of the dawn.

A fruit-seller's canvas softens my fall. I tear it and fall into a sea of tomatoes.

Alvise looks out of the window, fearing the worst.

"Sammy! Did you hurt yourself?"

I gaze up at him from the tomatoes.

"He whose name cannot be uttered" has kindly kept the joke within limits. No, I'm not hurt. Nevertheless, I feel that he is really overdoing things.

Alvise and von Kramer are strolling together along the treelined paths in the garden of the Sultana. The maestro has a cast on his foot.

Alvise is chatting with him affectionately, and von Kramer listens with his head bowed, nodding with resignation and humility.

I watch them nervously from my window. Yes, because dear old Franz has tried it again. Yes, "von Kill-myself" threw himself off Marrakesh's ancient city wall, and only broke a fibula. Not content, the obstinate Maestro "von *Je suis perdu*" tried again with barbiturates, following it up with a drug overdose. The next day, Alvise arrived just in time to keep "von *C'est la fin*" from hanging himself with a lady's black stocking. For now, it seems he's given up. Sure! So many failures cause bitterness and impotence. It is obvious that the real suicide for "von *Auf Wiedersehen–Tout est fini*" is to face the wrinkles, withered skin and sagging limbs of old age. How has Alvise behaved with him? Magnificently, of course. There's no use denying the fact that Alvise now appears to me in a different light. Not because of the old asshole, an almost trivial detail, but because the meeting with von Kramer makes me think over the idea that lit up in luminous letters in my mind at the club, when I saw the way Alvise was watching the male belly dancer.

Remember? "God of the oceans and heavens . . . please let Alvise . . ."

Of course, I was drunk that famous night. But now, with a clear mind, I continue thinking about it.

I convince myself it can't be anything but that. Yeah, come on! Isn't it strange that Alvise brings me with him all over the world? Why not? Think about it! It might seem odd and unexpected, but not impossible. In fact, it's highly probable. Maybe elementary and sensational. Dorothea, who knows him well, had said Alvise is in love with me.

I keep remembering Alvise's looks, Alvise's smiles, Alvise's melancholy moments, his tenderness, his affection. The more I think about it, the more I am certain of it. It would explain many things, and it would also give me the satisfaction of having a weapon at hand.

After so many trials and tribulations, "He whose name cannot be uttered" might have finally decided to grant me this favor, this prize! Perhaps I'll be able to see the super-perfect crack and maybe even cry and beg at my feet.

I could make him suffer, humiliate him. Maybe lead him to desperation, to suicide. Even make him die of consumption like Violetta.

After all, don't all fruits dream of being *La Traviata–La Dame aux Camélias? "Tout est fini!* Or *tutto fini"?* Of course! Sure! Whores, but ill and in love. Erotic creatures, but pure, good and humiliated by their sin of loving—unrepentant Magdalens, who loved not wisely but too well. Too generous with their thighs and hearts. They're all symbols of something else anyway. Who knows how Freud would explain this desire for *La Dame aux Camélias?* Who knows what he would read into those who hide behind the symbolic rôles? The father in *La Dame aux Camélias* might stand for the wife of your bisexual lover who comes to beg the *homme fatal* to keep everything quiet to avoid a scandal.

Scandal. Although today, kids don't give a damn about scandals, and it's been proven that bisexual fathers are much more generous with weekly allowances! Well, that is, as long as a remnant of guilt remains, and as long as it isn't taken away by a free society or psychoanalysis.

It's always better to have a father with a guilt complex! At least they're reasonable. Open to blackmail. You can have a genuine human relationship with them.

Could it be that I see something of my father in Alvise? Bullshit! Let's forget this psychoanalytical stuff! To horse, to horse! My gallant friend! I have to get down to business. This new insight has made things much more interesting.

Not only do I want Alvise's head now, I also want it devastated by love. The ginger of the erotic quotient is added to the soup, now grown tasteless with time, failure and my own vengeance.

In fact, I am sitting in front of my typewriter, but my eyes don't leave those two in the garden for a moment. I am making a big decision. Tonight I'll stake all. I want to set a trap.

If Alvise falls for it, I'll play with him like a cat with a mouse.

Taking advantage of the break in the conference, I

request a quiet dinner at home. "Yeah! Throw off your veil! Beneath your flawless guise of a prophet, you are hiding a weak spot, an 'Alvise's heel'—a little heart vibrating with love for me. For my beast, my orangutan, my condor. I'll fix you tonight!"

Alvise, unaware of what is about to befall him, puts his arm around von Kramer's and smiles.

Yeah! "Till tonight, dear limp-wristed prophet!"

The famous African night, with its aromas of orange blossoms and bougainvillea, purrs outside my window. The night is a black cat in heat, with half-closed, green and feline eyes. The night is licking its lips outside my Moorish Salome-room, full of shadows and shimmering lights.

"Night, night, my big cat purring outside the window, don't betray me, you won't betray me . . ." Alvise appears at the doorway giving onto the terrace. He is wearing a sumptuous dressing gown like something out of *The Son of the Sheik.*

It was a striking apparition. Like Rudolph Valentino or Theda Bara. He looks like a desert marauder.

Well, I have to admit that it isn't a bad start.

I whistle with admiration.

"Oh, Sheik, you here?"

Alvise laughs.

"You look like a mannequin in a Halston window, entitled: 'Tuareg lingerie'!"

Alvise laughs again.

He is laughing, not smiling! Good. Perhaps things are ripe. He is letting himself go. Who knows if the inscrutable ways of "He whose name cannot be uttered" are finally converging toward my long-coveted goal?

"Nice, isn't it? There's one for you as well. Haven't you seen it?"

He opens a chest of drawers built into the fretwork screen inlaid with mother-of-pearl. He pulls out another splendid gold-spangled Moorish caftan.

I whistle.

"Hey, are they given out to all the guests? Wow! And you're the one who criticizes me about consumerism and *having*, for a couple of measly television sets. And what do you say to your friend, the owner of the house?"

"Rather too much, actually. He's Mazarin's son. He's the King of Morocco's cousin who married the king of tin's daughter. I said so many things to them that they both ended up in a Tibetan convent. They live naked. On a handful of rice a day."

Alvise pushes me behind a screen.

"Come on. Put it on."

Hell! What grace. A real charmer. That subtle perfume that emanates from him. Yeah, they really know how to lay it on.

"Are they happy?"

"Who?"

"The King of Morocco and the queen of tin, with their handful of rice. Are they happy?"

"The last time I heard from them, they were in the midst of a mystical crisis. Everything considered, I'd say, yes, they seemed less unhappy. If they came out of their existential, philosophical-religiosity and back to the world, and took care of, for example, infant mortality in India, they'd definitely be happier."

Alvise looks out on the moonlit terrace. He breathes in the perfumed air.

I come out from behind the screen, looking like a stuffed doll. I am wearing the robe.

"Salaam aleichum!"

Alvise bows to me.

"Gorgeous, aren't they? They're nuptial robes. Shall we go to dinner?"

Did he say nuptial? Ah, he really slipped up there.

"Sure, it's better than a double-breasted gray flannel suit!"

"Much better! They really follow the cult of masculine beauty in these places. They exalt it. You look great in that."

He said it. He compromised himself by paying me a physical compliment.

I look at my reflection in the mirror, and I appear to myself—yes!—simply and absolutely disgusting.

It is an enchanting evening. We sit cross-legged around a low table that is set with exquisite little cups and saucers. The garden of the Sultana is intoxicating us with its sensual aromas. The servants finish serving the coffee and a yellow liqueur.

Alvise raises a cup.

"To your book."

"To my book . . . and to the two of us."

I swallow the liqueur and gaze at Alvise languidly. I have eaten and drunk quite a bit, and I am feeling excited and dangerous. I stare at Alvise: "Yes, little pansy, I'm sure you'll soon be begging for it! And I'll be waiting for you."

Alvise looks up at the starry sky. I voluptuously breathe in the perfumed air.

"What a night!"

"Let's take a walk."

We get up and begin to stroll slowly through the garden. I lean on Alvise's shoulder.

"The scent of these orange blossoms really goes to your head. Don't you think so? The famous tropical sky."

Alvise looks up again.

"Mmm . . . Mmmm."

He acts as if nothing is happening, but I can see that he is worried. It is obvious what it is. I persist.

"The stars are reflected in your eyes. You have beautiful eyes. I never realized it before."

Alvise lights a cigarette.

"Do you want to tell me about your novel?"

Now we are climbing up the large staircase that leads to the white colonnade lined with delicate pillars and colorful tiles. I sigh.

"I don't feel like it. This night is so . . . so languid, so sensual. These aromas have filled me with desire."

Alvise smiles.

"That reminds me of an old Neapolitan song."

He bursts into song. His voice is beautiful.

"'Na smania . . . 'n'ipocondria . . . 'na voglia 'e chissà che . . ."

I squint at him.

"Ah! This I didn't know. You even sing well. You're just extraordinary! You know, I wouldn't be surprised if you could leap from wing to wing in the Metropolitan

Opera House like Nijinsky, or Mikhail Baryshnikov in *Le Spectre de la Rose!* Tell me the truth. Do you know how to dance too?"

"No, come on. What are you doing, making fun of me?"

"No. It's just that you're so unusual. You're . . ."

"Stop talking about me. It's a subject that doesn't interest me!"

"Sorry. It's just that, here . . . I don't know. It must be the garden. I must have some kind of hay fever. You know, with all these scents. Maybe it's the pollen, who knows? This heat . . . I'm all sweaty. See? You don't even sweat. You should go to the doctor. Why is it you don't sweat? It could be a disease, instead of a semi-divine attribute. Maybe some form of juvenile acne. I mean, after all . . ."

"You're strange tonight, unsettled. What is it?"

"Well, I don't know. I feel a desire for something. But, you know, it might even be indigestion. It might be a need for love. One thing I can tell you, this Arab cuisine sure is spicy. I feel like they performed *The Sabre Dance* on my tongue. But you . . . You're so handsome, and so relaxed. All right, all right. We won't talk about you. There is a special atmosphere in this place—it seems like almost anything could happen."

We are now out on the elaborate balcony that lies outside our bedrooms. Alvise slows down in front of his room.

"Well, I'm going to bed. Good night."

"So soon? No, wait. You can't do that right after an Arab dinner. You risk spending the night dreaming of green lizards. Let's at least drink something first. I've got some excellent whiskey."

I insist and push Alvise into my room. Salome dances in the painting on the wall.

I pour out the whiskey with a trembling hand as I watch Alvise gazing at the watercolor. Then, he turns and looks at the papers on the desk where I have begun working on my novel.

"Ah! Then you started writing your novel."

"Oh, just the outline. One night in Rome, something happened. I had a flash of insight, but now I'm having trouble developing it. You . . . You could help me."

"Well, I've been trying to for a month now. For what it's worth."

I recline erotically and seductively on the bed.

"You could. You could help me a lot, while I . . . You know, I think about it often during our travels. What am I to you? Nothing? Something trivial? Maybe even a pain in the ass?"

Alvise raises his glass of whiskey.

"What are you saying, Sammy? You're a friend. I'm deeply fond of you, you know."

I roll over on the bed like a clumsy whore. Then I leer at him lasciviously.

"How deeply?"

Alvise smiles.

"Come on, Sammy. Let's not behave like children."

"You're right! We're not children. Okay, just forget it!"

Now I put on a hurt expression. I'm plastered, dammitall. I really drank too much, but maybe it's better that way. I can overcome all complexes, and loosen the brakes of my inhibitions. I sit up on the bed and pout.

"Jesus Christ, Sammy. What's wrong? You're so touchy. Believe me, I hate to see you suffer."

I arch my eyebrows. "Suffer?" Alvise always succeeds in astounding me. What could he mean? I am really annoyed. I feel that the game isn't going according to plan. I whirl around angrily.

"Me, suffer? But I'm not suffering at all. Look, I really couldn't give less of a shit!"

Alvise smiles.

"Of course. Our friendship is what's important. That's sacred. I care for you very much, Sammy. You're a friend, a poet, a sensitive human being. That's why I wanted so much to be with you. You'll see, you'll get over it. Perhaps you already have."

Atrocious suspicion. What is this *schmuck* saying?!

"What are you saying? What do you mean, I'll get over it? Just what am I supposed to get over? What are you talking about?"

I am green in the face. A hand begins to twist my intestines. I'm still not sure I understand him. I look like an idiot.

"You don't have to have any hang-ups with me. I've sensed it for a long time now; also because you did everything you could to make me realize it. Your always wanting to be with me—without anyone else around, the way you look at me. It's not because of your tendencies. I certainly won't be the one to criticize them. On the contrary. Why, look at Michelangelo, Proust, Gide . . . In fact, I'm the one who looks a little ridiculous. You don't know how I wish I were more free about it, because, I know, it is a limitation, an unnatural reserve, and even a sort of prejudice. It's also stupid and bourgeois. Nature doesn't have these silly rules. It's not that I'm prejudiced, it's just that I'm not inclined that way. Even with Franz, whom I loved like a brother, it was a tragedy. Then I understood. It is something beyond my nature. Anyway, I'm sorry I can't return your sentiment. I'm just very boring and ordinary."

I feel the blood rising to my ears. A deafening rage is building up inside of me. I jump up on the bed like a ferocious samurai.

"Oh, no, *bubeleh!* You've got it all wrong. What are you doing, turning the tables now? You're telling me *I'm* the faggot? Oh, no! Fuck that! *You're* the one who's the faggot, not me. *You* are the faggot. You sniveling, queer little fruitcake!"

Alvise is shocked by my rage.

"Try and calm down. I'm sorry to see you in this state. I was wrong, sorry. I only wanted to help you. Don't act like that."

"I'll act like this and worse! You wanna pass the faggot shit off on me?!"

"No, no. I didn't want to do that at all. On the contrary. I see you're beside yourself. You're hysterical. Maybe it's because of my refusal."

"Your refusal? What refusal? I'm the one who's refusing you, because you disgust me! You're nothing but a fruity homo pederast! And if you're not, you're impotent or worse. Because your wife is so sex-starved that I had to give her what she wanted!"

Alvise gets very angry.

"You've lost your head, and you're getting vulgar. Leave Dorothea out of it. She has nothing to do with this business!"

"I won't leave anything out, you bastard! Stupid queer, you and your nymphomaniac wife! And 'He whose name cannot be uttered,' who's playing on your side!"

By this time, I was shrieking like a banshee.

"Sammy. Sammy. Try to calm down. I didn't want to hurt you."

"But I did! I not only wanted to hurt you, I wanted to kill you!"

With a leap, I grab a pistol from a panoply of antique silver and steel weapons which hangs over a leopard skin on the wall.

"What are you doing? Put away that pistol!"

"No! Because I still want to! Yes!"

I aim the pistol at Alvise after having raised the silver arabesqued firing pin.

"Put that pistol away. Stop it, Sammy."

"No, I've got to kill you. 'He whose name cannot be uttered' knows why, because I explained it all to him. And if you don't understand why now, he'll explain it to you afterward. Anyway, you'll have all of eternity! I have to kill you, dear Alvise Ottolenghi Portaleoni, Isaac Smith, prophet of peace, Nobel Prize winner, Amnesty International son-of-a-bitch. I need your head, because, you see, when you say that all men are equal, you're lying. Because there are men, and then there's you. You, Alvise. Did you ever realize what you're like? Did you know the damage someone like you does to someone like me? You, who preach nonviolence. Did you know I was a normal, tranquil, contented man until I met you again? Since you came back into my life, I've felt like a poor, underdeveloped *schmuck*. A failure, a charity case. I feel like a worm.

"Do you realize that someone like you makes a normal person feel lousy? Why should they have to measure up to your fucking perfection? Your *being*, your embarrassing goodness, your boundless altruism, your superior culture, your goddam detachment from earthly goods? You son-of-a-bitch! You, who go around giving away inheritances and donating your income to worthy causes. Big fucking deal! You can still go on living like a millionaire as the guest of cardinals and princes, in palaces and villas. That's why you don't need the little vulgar symbols of ownership, so important to the masses who sell their souls to the consumer society for a color TV, a car, a plastic prefab house. They offer you everything on a silver platter. And you don't even have to pay taxes. You don't have to kiss any boss's ass.

"It's easy for you, *bube!* Just one look from your magnetic eyes and the girls rip their panties off. They jump into your bed and fall in love with you forever. World leaders bow their heads, repressing their desire to kiss your feet in homage. Cardinals weep because they can't make you Pope. And you sail on, soaring over our wretchedness, preaching perfection.

"For two thousand years, the Catholics have been wondering why anyone would crucify Christ! He got on everybody's nerves with his sublimity, his superior *being*.

So what are the rest of us—little worms? Well, then leave us little worms alone. Doesn't a man have the right to feel that he is a man? A man can't feel like a *schmuck* just because of you. The very fact that you exist, your being here, is monstrous and unjust. You're the devil. You're the poison of the world. You're the root of all evil!"

Alvise listens patiently to all the madness that spills from my lips. He is deeply stricken by what he hears.

"Yes, maybe. Maybe you're right."

"No! Don't tell me I'm right! Don't tell me I'm right, you super-perfect monster! Son-of-a-bitch! Telling me I'm right is too much! I've got to extinguish your sublimity!"

I fumble with the trigger.

"Careful, it could be loaded."

"Let's hope so."

I fire the gun. Yes, I finally fire it!

Alvise is hit. With a look of startled horror in his eyes, and a scream of surprise, he drops to the ground.

I stand there frozen, with the pistol in my hand. I am shocked.

I look up toward the possible dwelling place of "He whose name cannot be uttered."

I did it. I killed him!

Incredible!

The music from Salome bursts loudly over Alvise's body as his nightingale blood begins to stain the Moorish carpet.

I can't believe it. My feet go wild around Alvise's pale, still face. No, I am not dancing. It is a fit of terror that is driving me mad.

I try to clean the pistol. The bright red color is making my head spin. I force myself to get rid of all the traces. Then I look up at the watercolor and back at Alvise, I become fully aware of what I've done. With a stifled cry of horror, I tear out of the room.

I hear Salome behind me with the triumphant sound of Strauss's music: dancing the dance of destiny, love and death with her swirling veils.

I trip, fall and get up again, and disappear into the perfumed African night. Oh, that rotten, perfidious cat.

Sky. A plane in the sky. The airport.

I go up to the TWA counter, heavily disguised in Arab clothing. I wear a burnoose over my head to cover most of the recognizable parts of my face. A pair of black sunglasses can just be glimpsed through the folds of my headdress. My desire to remain incognito is intense. I disguise my voice. I used to be good at it.

"New York, please."

The Arab behind the counter looks at me.

"Everything is booked till—hey!"

He stares at me, and then a smile spreads over his face.

"You're . . . Oh, Mr. Silverman. Hey, Mike Bullit is tops, Sam!"

He pulls out a paperback mystery in Arabic with my photo on the back. I've been recognized on the first go. Oh, well!

It might cost me the electric chair, but at least I get a place. You also have to look at the good side of things. Yeah. Only it isn't easy finding the good side of this situation. But it sure is easy finding the ridiculous side! An Edgar Prize winner for the best thrillers, a master of mystery and intrigue (all set with his attaché case packed full of six schemes for a perfect crime), has gone and committed the most imperfect crime imaginable. Fingerprints were left all over the place. I even left my bags behind, with my address and everything. It is enough to skip the trial altogether and go straight to the chair like an express train. The electric chair, that's all I'd need. What a disgrace, especially from a professional point of view. The expert in perfect crime should look like an incredible asshole! Such stupidity is enough to drive you to commit suicide out of shame! Mike Bullit—suddenly a shithead. A series of blunders, one imbecility after another. It is enough to make you sink into a total crisis! And just what does the asshole decide to do? Instead of committing hara-kiri, or hanging himself in the plane's toilet, he is busy writing!

I am writing my famous book. In fact, I am almost vomiting it, neurotically. Four chapters are already written. I am having a fit, I am hysterical.

Of course, I am free at last! My rage has finally exploded! I got Alvise's head. Now I can be an artist. Now I can renounce all earthly goods. Perhaps even give up the color TV on the day of the World Series.

Now I understand: *Having* is some sort of consolation for not *being*. But, I finally *am*.

It's not *cogito ergo sum* but "I kill Alvise, *ergo sum.*" My liberty explodes like a river thundering over a collapsed dam. The fruits of vengeance are sweet. It is marvelous.

My writing is fluid and inspired like that of the great

authors. It is better than if it had been written by dear, departed Alvise, the Nobel shit-winner!

It is obvious: "He whose name cannot be uttered" is finally on my side. He understands me. He guides my hand and my head. He protects me.

As I write, the airplane descends, and I can see New York from above, with the old Statue of Liberty and the Brooklyn Bridge. I keep on writing and writing.

A fisherman is peacefully fishing beneath the Brooklyn Bridge.

An old, leather-faced tramp passes by in a small boat with some sacks. The two men wave at each other. Then the old man pulls up to a dock and hands a large bucket to the fisherman.

"Here, take it."

"Thanks, Tom."

"And these too."

He hands him a stack of newspapers.

"How's our friend?"

He nods over to a corrugated metal shack that stands in an abandoned lot by the riverbank.

"Is he still here?"

The fisherman nods.

"Yep."

Tom looks over at the shack with curiosity.

"Must be hidin' there because of somethin', huh?"

"He says he's writing a book about a wanted guy who's in hiding."

"Well, I think he's gotta be in trouble or somethin'."

"Maybe, but he sure does write like crazy. From morning to night. I guess he's nuts."

There is a little window in the shack through which you can see inside. There I am, thickly bearded, sitting with a blanket over my shoulders. I am writing frenetically.

You know what I am writing? "The end." I have a large pile of papers in front of me. It is my novel. With a hurrah, I get up and raise my finger in a vulgar gesture.

"Up yours, Alvise! It's finished. Hurray!"

I stretch out and yawn. I contemplate my pile of papers with satisfaction, then solemnly put them away in an old cardboard box. Life is great. I am feeling hungry.

I go over to the little window and look out at the sky.

A bum is sneaking along the side of a brownstone that once was the coveted residence of Sammy Silverman, the master of thrillers and the creator of Mike Bullit.

He looks like an old drunk from the Bowery, with his thick beard, a pair of black sunglasses, a scruffy hat and a dirty coat with its collar turned up. Yes, it's *me*.

I look around furtively and hide among the bushes in the garden. I have to be very cautious because I don't want to fall into any traps.

Now that my novel is finished, it is time to face reality. Instinct tells me to be on my guard. Things are too calm. It's strange that I haven't heard anything about the death of Alvise during the twenty days I spent hiding in the shack. There was a total silence. A Nobel Prize winner, a member of Amnesty International—the crime is probably attributed to some terrorist organization, and therefore I, inevitably proven guilty, am considered a political terrorist. I wonder what those geniuses in the

FBI came up with. Then the business probably passed to the CIA and an international anti-terrorist organization. Just think what those guys must have come up with, the world situation being the way it is. Therefore it is top secret. Now the trap is set. They are all waiting for me to stick my head in it.

And I have a great desire to stick my head in it too. That's why I just can't fight off my homesickness, despite all my precautions. I am scrambling around the garden and sneaking along the walls like a cat. I creep up to a window furtively and look in.

Alice is alone in my study, dusting my desk.

She lingers with my photograph in her hands; it's the one of me with the pipe and the scarf. I can't see her all that well, but I am sure that her eyes are filling up with tears.

My poor Alice. Of course she is crying. She loves me. My loving housewife, my companion, the mother of my children, the woman who makes me chicken soup when I have a cold. It breaks my heart to see her moving around so sadly in my study. I have such a strong desire to run in there and take her into my arms, the darling little nitwit. The telephone suddenly rings. She answers it. What is she doing now? Hey, is she laughing? Ah, so that's the way it is. I knew it! That's what you get for trusting broads. She is giggling away. I am dying to go in there. But it is impossible.

It has to be the cheese in the trap. Of course, the house has to be under surveillance. They probably installed microphones. The children have been sent away. It's clear, with a wicked murderer for a father. The marksmen with their precision rifles are probably already positioned. Yeah, I'd have to be pretty stupid to walk into a trap like that.

I hide in the bushes again. Something unexpectedly hits me that makes me cry out in pain.

"Owwwww!"

Chucky and Chipper are at the basement window, shooting things at me with their phosphorescent plastic moon-guns.

"Scram, you dirty, stinkin' robber!"

"Mammmaaaa, Mammaaa, there's a robber in the garden!"

I fling myself over the fence and scuttle off like a rat.

Alice is shopping in a five and ten in a crowd of people and carts.

A telephone rings in a booth by the counter. A check-out clerk answers it and looks around. As he holds the receiver to his ear, he studies the customers. Then he calls out to one of them.

"Hey! Is there a Mrs. Silverman here? Telephone."

"For me?"

The clerk, who is the boss's brother-in-law, shakes his head and grumbles.

"Now they get calls in the stores while they do their shopping. This world is getting screwier every second."

Alice runs to the telephone, looking worried.

"Hello?"

I am in a phone booth out in the street. I put a handkerchief and a scarf over the receiver and make my voice unrecognizable.

"Hello?"

Alice's face lights up in the store.

"Sammy! It's you! Finally. You've had me so worried. Everybody's been looking for you like crazy."

Damn her. She recognized me right away.

"Yes, I know. But talk low, dammitall!"

"Where are

"Nearby. Tell me, ..

"I should tell you? You tell me. You're the one who left town. Nothing's new at home. Everything is just the same. What's happened to you?"

"Never mind. Tell me who's looking for me."

"A lot of people have called. Your publisher, the TV repairman, your aunt in Oregon, Mr. Farth."

"What about the police? Haven't the police been looking for me?"

"No, why?"

"Forget it."

"Your publisher, Nick, is looking for you especially. He phoned personally. He said he needs to see you urgently. He said: 'The minute you see him, tell him to come and see me. There's big news for him.' And he also asked me not to let you talk to anyone else before you see him. Anyway, nothing makes sense."

Ah! That's it. I listen to her carefully.

"So. He said for me not to talk to anyone else? Hmm. Listen, Alice. You've got to promise me you won't talk to anyone, not even the children. You haven't heard from me. Is that clear? You don't know anything about me!"

"What the hell for, Sammy? You're scaring me to death."

"Alice, don't start being a pain. I'll tell you about it afterward."

"Afterward? After what? Look, Sammy, I'm really fed up with all of this! I'm not putting up with it anymore. Where the hell are you? What the hell's happened to you? I'm even a little curious, and you know why! In fact, look, if you don't tell me where you are, you know what I'm gonna do? I'll go straight to the police."

"Always blackmailing. You're a vicious bitch! All right, you win."

The little boat tugs along under the Brooklyn Bridge, carrying Alice to my refuge.

I watch her from the window in my shack. As the boat draws closer, I can see that she is troubled and frightened. I'm sure she's never traveled on the East River before. Her face is pale and she is sneezing constantly.

The boat pulls up to the bank and dips dangerously because Alice is having trouble getting out. The old tramp accompanies her to my shack.

She sees me at the door. She freezes at the sight of my thick, long beard, the scruffy hat and the bizarre rags that I wear. Her eyes widen and fill up with tears. Then she bursts out crying.

I am furious. I pull her into the shack right away.

"Cut it out. Come on, Alice. Don't make yourself conspicuous. You can go now, Tom, thanks."

I slam the door behind us.

"Cut it out."

Alice tries to get a hold of herself. She speaks like a child, between sniffs and sobs. She has the same little voice that made me call her "Alice in Wonderland."

"Oh, Sammy, what's happened to you, darling? You look like you've gone insane. Why are you here in this place? Everybody's waiting for you at home. The study is ready. Sammy, what's happening to you?"

Her curiosity is getting on my nerves.

"Nothing. Nothing. Dammit, Alice, I had things to do. Anyway, tell me about the house. Have people been looking for me?"

Naturally, she isn't listening to me. She seems like one of Chekhov's characters, the kind you ask "What time is it?" and they answer "To Moscow, to Moscow!" I mean, each person goes rambling on without listening to the other.

"Have you become an alcoholic?"

"Don't talk crap. Are you sure the police haven't been looking for me?"

She continues. Instead of answering me, she asks questions.

"Are you in trouble with drugs?"

I could kill her!

"Why don't you answer me, instead of asking stupid questions?"

Now she loses her temper.

"What do you mean, stupid questions, you bastard! Darling, you're killing me. Now you tell me what happened, or else I'm going to start screaming."

Our dialogue is getting out of hand. Even the best of men have to exercise a little patience.

"All right. Swear on the children that you won't tell anyone."

"On the children? You're a monster. All right, I swear!"

The moment has come. I look at the seagulls who carelessly fly under the famous bridge which owes its fame to Arthur Miller and an Italian brand of chewing gum. The seagulls glide through the air with their outstretched wings. The sound of traffic becomes muffled. A distant tugboat sounds its foghorn. The sky is gray, so is the water. A long pause. Then I say it.

"I killed Alvise."

"Huh?"

"I killed Alvise."

She doesn't believe me.

"Alvise? No!"

"Yes."

Alice is stricken. Then she slowly begins to cry. Tears roll down her cheeks as if she'd turned on two faucets.

"Oh, Sammy."

I look down on her from the untouchable heights of my criminality. I am far away from her. After all, I am a murderer!

"I not only killed him, but I did it in the stupidest way, leaving proof, traces, fingerprints and even my luggage with my business cards! So they know very well that it was me. They may even think it's too easy. They probably think I'm a terrorist connected with the Iranians or the Arabs. That's why nothing leaked out in the press or on TV. They must have prepared a trap for me. You understand? Because they must have thought it was a plot, a political crime, who knows? You know how it is over in that part of the world. It's such a mess. Do you realize what I'm saying? It's not normal. They didn't even publicize his death. Who knows what they're thinking? You can imagine the CIA with all their big brains. And, after all, the fact that Alvise was in the Middle East and in Israel. He was a Nobel Prize winner. The implications are staggering. The investigation must be carried out behind a veil of strict secrecy. I'm sure they went to see Nick at the publishing house. That's why he told you not to talk. It's a coded message . . . for me. He wants to tell me something. Oh, I know Nick all right. He'd sell his mother on her deathbed in installments if he could hit it big. He found out about everything. Of course! You'll see, he'll want to offer me a hiding place in the Bahamas in exchange for the exclusive rights to the blow-by-blow account of the crime. Sure, that's it. Think about it: An Edgar Prize winner liquidates a Nobel Prize winner, sharing the same publisher. It's a fabulous deal for him! And he still doesn't even know that there's a golden motive behind it. An Edgar Prize winner bumps off a Nobel Prize winner for a novel. A novel worthy of the Nobel Prize. This one here."

I caress my papers that lie in the cardboard shoe box.

"Alice. Think! It'll be the biggest advertising campaign in the history of publishing, since the very beginning—when they wrote on tablets. It's got to be that way. You'll see."

Alice is listening to me with wide eyes. I am very excited.

"And I've thought it over. He's the only one who'd have any interest in helping me. You understand that?"

Alice shakes her head. Her eyes are brimming with tears.

"No, I don't understand anything. Are you sure you're feeling all right?"

"Alice, I really missed you a lot, but fuck off! Don't you see I'm fine? I haven't felt so great in months."

"Maybe you've really gone insane, Sammy. Are you sure you killed Alvise?"

"Alice, I love you, but quit acting like an asshole. You're the wife of an unusual man. You've got to be up to snuff. Until today, we've played at the idea of *having*—having stupid objects, identifying ourselves with the TV, with the car, with your mink . . ."

"Oh, God! What've you got against my mink now? There, right away with my mink. With all this mess you've made, why are you picking on my mink?"

"No, that's not it. I meant that I'm another man, Alice. I don't want to *have*. I want to *be*, and now I can *be*, see? To *be!* And you must also *be*. You must especially *be* up to snuff. And you may one day accompany me to Stockholm, when I go and claim the Nobel Prize."

She continues gaping at me with her tear-filled eyes.

"Oh, Sammy. Something's really turned your head."

"Yes, Alice, something sure did turn my head."

"No offense, but it looks like you've got delusions of grandeur. You're acting like a megalomaniac."

I smile. I have to be patient with her. She'll eventually understand.

"Well, Alice, this is only the beginning. You've got to prepare yourself! You're the wife of a murderer."

"Oh, God!"

"Yes, but a great one. Perhaps a genius."

"Sammy . . ."

I give her a little pinch on the cheek.

"Careful. Now you and I will go to the publisher's. I'll go up and see Nick. You wait down in the car by the emergency exit. Be ready, and keep the motor running in case we have to make a sudden getaway."

She still doesn't understand. Fear is growing within me, but I also find strength. I feel I am growing in stature as Alice goes on sputtering.

"Oh, Sammy. I'm no good at that kind of thing. I . . . I wouldn't want . . . Oh, Sammy! Our life seemed so peaceful before."

I am feeling superior.

"Yes, it seemed nice, but it was full of shit. It's over for good and all. Everything has changed. Let's go, baby. The great adventure's just beginning."

"I'm scared, Sammy."

"Me too."

Here I am, walking down the corridor in the publishing house. The secretaries, who have always been my accomplices, run to meet me.

They haven't seen me in a long time, and they smile and greet me warmly. Especially Mia, who is blond and shapely and has rhythmic tits—I mean in the sense that when she walks, one bumps against the other on the upbeat and makes you want to dance the samba. God bless her. I always promised her that someday I'd drag her out on the terrace at the end of the corridor and make whoopie, and show her how to samba to the beat of the rush-hour traffic. She has a weakness for me. Since she seems to know what's going on, like Zarathustra, I wink and smile at her. She accompanies me and whispers:

"Hey, you're looking good. You're really macho like that. Wow! Come on. The boss is waiting for you. Looks like there's big news. That beard really looks good on you. You look like a rock star." And with a smile of complicity, she opens the door to the boss's office.

Nick is sitting like a toad behind his massive desk. A fat cigar hangs from his lips, and he looks like he's in his usual bad mood. When he sees me, however, he raises his eyebrows and attempts a smile, which turns out to be more of a smirk. He assumes an air which is halfway between bored and suitable for the occasion.

"Hey, is that really you? How ya doin', Sam? You finally came back. But you've changed. You look like a rock star. Where did you disappear to?"

I don't answer.

Central Park can be seen thirty floors below us, beyond the smoky plate-glass windows. The tall treetops sway softly in the Atlantic breeze. The great park is a splash of green in the concrete heart of the most powerful city of the modern world. Traffic flows around it in a constant, implacable, obsessive rhythm, to the beat of traffic lights.

Oppressive rain and thunder clouds hang low over the city. New York, New York, my crazy, confusing, irreplaceable old home. When you are so dark and threatening, it seems as if you are holding up those skyscrapers, those big, black clouds, and I like you even more.

Yes, I hope to pay tribute to you, dear old town. If

this game with Destiny comes to a conclusion, as seems possible, if "He whose name cannot be uttered" keeps his protective hand over me, I dedicate my novel to you. To New York!

Seagulls soar low through the air, grazing the smoky windows with their wings.

Nick isn't used to my Brando-*Viva Zapata*-like pauses. With an expression of amazement, he follows my gaze to see if there's something interesting outside. Naturally, New York is still there, with seagulls and park, so he doesn't see anything. He turns around and offers me a cigar.

"Well? *Cherchez la femme?* Please, I don't want to know anything, even if the police are after you."

I look at him.

"Trying to be funny?"

Nick smiles. He is warmhearted and friendly. He must have been really upset, and since he is such a bad actor, he is overdoing his calm appearance.

"We filled the monthly publication with a new edition of *Mike Bullit Returns to Chinatown.* Remember that one? Well, it was a big hit! In fact we're also going to reissue *The Dragon with the Jade Eyes* to follow it up. But these are only details. Hold onto your seat, Sam. This is going to be a historic moment."

He pulls a pile of papers out from a drawer.

"What is that? A warrant for my arrest?"

Then I take a better look at it.

"Hey, it looks like a contract. Is it a contract?"

Nick tries to be patient.

"It's a contract."

He shoves it under my nose. I smile. There it is. I am an absolute genius. I had foreseen it all correctly.

"I thought so. Only I know you, Nick. You're cynical, but quick and on the ball. You've got eyes like a hawk. From way up here, you don't let the prey get away. You aim for it and pounce on it."

"I don't know what you're talking about. Come on. Look it over, read it and sign it."

I begin to read.

I stop halfway through. I nearly have a heart attack.

I stare at Nick, who is sitting there in his cigar smoke, looking more like a toad than ever.

"A book for the series *The Great Masterpieces?* For me? I don't get it, Nick. You're offering me a contract for . . . Explain it to me."

"I suspected you didn't know how to write, but not knowing how to read is just ridiculous! Come on, Sam. It's written in triplicate. Little money, but a lot of prestige. We'd be making a leap in the dark. Wasn't this what you wanted? Look, isn't it true that you were getting fed up with writing mysteries and that you had literary aspirations worthy of the Nobel Prize? So, sign it and then go out and get drunk."

I continue looking at him without understanding what is happening. I smell a rat. Something doesn't make sense.

"You didn't want the exclusive rights for what happened? You wanted this instead?"

I push the shoe box over to Nick. Nick stares at it and then begins to read. He looks up at me.

"What is this?"

"You're joking. It's a novel worthy of the Nobel Prize. Mine."

"Jesus Christ! You've already written it! Look, I don't get it."

"*I* don't get it."

"Well, let's try to get things straight. Because, to be honest, I've got very little to do with this. But when the big guys get into it, you've got to pay attention to them."

Just then, a little bell rings. The door opens. Nick nods to the secretary. She steps aside and makes way for . . . Alvise!

Alvise is alive! He is smiling. He has a plaster cast on his arm.

Nick stands up and shows him to a seat, with a great deal of respect.

"Here we are. Your protégé finally stuck his head out the door and came back to Mamma, Professor. He did everything, Sammy. He almost had to rape me."

I say:

"Hello."

But I think no sound comes out.

I am suddenly seized by an imperceptible tremor. Alvise gives me a sweet, understanding look. Nick goes on talking.

"I like to have things out in the open. I feel that you are a great writer of thrillers, which may well be a minor form of literature but is the oxygen of the publishing trade! When a Nobel Prize winner like the professor comes along . . . You see, Mr. Isaac Smith Ottolenghi Portaleoni is convinced that you're a great, neglected writer. He says we have a duty to launch you. I don't want the remorse of having suffocated a genius. Here's the contract. Sign it. What are you waiting for?"

I look over at Alvise. He is still smiling. There's a way to describe that kind of smile. Ah, yes—sublime.

"Fantastic. You've written it."

He goes over to the manuscript Nick has taken out of the box.

"Wonderful. You were right. I'm happy to have collaborated."

He taps his plastered arm allusively. He didn't die, he's only been wounded in the arm, that's all. Got that? His smile seems demoniacal. I am tense and immobile. Nick, who has the brutality of a rhinoceros, doesn't understand, and keeps insisting in a confident, pushy way.

"Come on, you jerk, sign it. Speechless, eh? You didn't expect it, did you? Well, you should put up a monument to Mr. Ottolenghi Portaleoni. He's your patron saint. Thank him."

I stand up. Everything explodes. A primitive sound like an elephant trumpeting fills the air.

"Noooooooo!"

And with a leap, I begin to do what I've been wanting to do for a long time. I land a powerful uppercut on Alvise's smiling chin.

Nick runs over to stop me, but I am like a wild beast, and nothing can hold me back.

I send Nick flying over his desk. Then I grab hold of Alvise. Nick gets on top of me again to hold me back. But I am strong and aroused.

I seize a heavy Tiffany lamp from the desk. The Tiffany lamp, Alvise, Nick and I all form a horrifying whirling carrousel. Impelled by centrifugal force, we lose our balance and spin off on a tangent.

The whirling carrousel with the three of us and the heavy Tiffany lamp strikes and shatters the crystal-glass windows on the thirtieth floor.

We all burst out into the sky of New York City.

Flying with the Tiffany lamp above me, among the fragments of glass and the scattered sheets of my manuscript, I glance around desperately, and I have just enough time to notice that Alvise, with his arm plastered like a teacup handle, has miraculously been caught on the pole of the American flag which hangs a few floors below.

He is saved. The injustice of "He whose name cannot be uttered" is atrocious! Shit! I can hear Alvise's desperate, loving voice, damn him!

"Sammy!!!"

The dirty pages of my manuscript are strewn under the wheels of the buses and cars that drive down Fifth Avenue along the park.

I am impaled on a branch of a huge tree. I am pierced through the chest.

I look like a puppet pinned against the sky. One eye is open, the other is closed, and I wear an expression of incredible rage. I am dead without a doubt.

The police have made a circle below, to keep the people away. Alvise, Alice and Dorothea stand within the circle looking up at me.

Alice is crying. Alvise is holding her tenderly against his chest as he gazes up toward the sky.

"To have or not to have. To be or not to be. Poor Sammy."

My cadaver suddenly delivers with an awful noise. You know that cadavers release air from all their orifices. It is my last duty. After all, a man is a man, even when he's dead!

Alvise continues talking to Alice.

"He lived a wonderful life."

"You must write his story, Alvise. I beg you. Write about my Sammy."

"Yes. I promise you, Alice, I'll write it."

Did you get that? What the fuck! Hell, no! He's liable to get another Nobel Prize, the opportunist pig!

The big branch that I am impaled on suddenly gives way with a terrible splitting sound.

The crowd screams. Body and branch fall to the ground with a resounding crash, right on top of Alvise.

Shit! Missed by a fraction of an inch!

The aim was good.

A fraction of an inch. Maybe they pulled him back, or maybe he jumped out of fear. Or perhaps "He whose name cannot be uttered" gave him a little push. Or perhaps it's luck, because Alvise has been saved by a hair.

Pale, handsome, unhurt Alvise looks at me—at me, a broken puppet lying in the mud at his feet.

I lost my last chance! Oh, yes! I've had it!

I won't play anymore.